Alexander McCall Smith is the author of
the bestselling No. 1 Ladies' Detective
Agency series. He has written over thirty
books for young readers, including two
other School Ship *Tobermory* adventures.

Iain McIntosh's illustrations have won
awards in the worlds of advertising, design
and publishing. He has illustrated many
of Alexander McCall Smith's books.

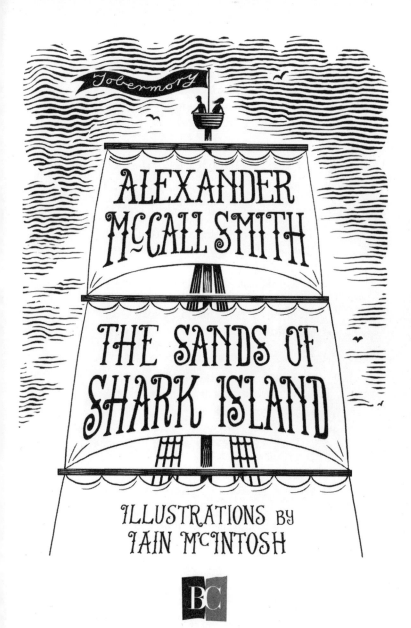

Tobermory

ALEXANDER McCALL SMITH

THE SANDS OF SHARK ISLAND

ILLUSTRATIONS BY
IAIN McINTOSH

BC

This edition first published in 2017 by
BC Books,
an imprint of Birlinn Limited
West Newington House
10 Newington Road
Edinburgh
EH9 1QS

www.bcbooksforkids.co.uk

First published in hardback in 2016

ISBN: 978 1 78027 441 6

British Library Cataloguing-in-Publication Data
A catalogue record for this book is available
from the British Library

Typeset by Mark Blackadder

Printed and bound by
Grafica Veneta, Italy
www.graficaveneta.com

THIS
BOOK
is for
ERIC

Ben MacTavish

Fee MacTavish

CHAPTER 1

A trip in the submarine

There were two reasons why Ben and Fee MacTavish were lucky. The first was that they were both students on the School Ship *Tobermory*, a school that was also a ship and that sailed all over the world. They had been sent there because their parents were well-known marine scientists and often had to be away from home on their research submarine.

"I'm afraid there are no schools under water," said their father. "So it's going to have to be somewhere up above!"

Ben and Fee were twins, and were both twelve. Fee liked to point out, though, that she was two minutes older than her brother – and that, she claimed, was important.

"Even two minutes can make a big difference," she said.

To which Ben – if he heard her saying that – would reply, "Nonsense!" Which is what he often said if his sister came up with some remark with which he disagreed. He always said *nonsense* in a polite way, of course, as he and Fee never argued and always agreed on most important matters, if not on everything.

The second reason why Ben and Fee were lucky was that they both had good friends, and these friends all got on well with one another, which is what most people hope their friends will do.

"It must be hard," Ben once said to his sister, "if you have a friend who doesn't like one of your other friends. What do you do then?"

Fee pondered this; she was glad this had never happened to her. "I suppose you make sure that you see them at different times," she said. "Perhaps you have morning friends and then you have afternoon friends. You'd see them separately that way."

"It's much easier if they all like one another," said Ben.

"Much easier," agreed Fee.

And who were Ben and Fee's special friends?

Well, in Ben's case it was Badger Tomkins, with whom he shared a cabin on the *Tobermory* on Middle Deck. Badger was an American boy who came from New York. His father and mother were successful business people who sent him away to school because they were too busy to give him much time. It made no difference to them if their son went to school in Scotland or America, or Timbuctoo, for that matter, as they hardly ever saw him anyway.

"I guess you can go where you like," said Badger's

Badger

father. "There are always plenty of planes."

Luckily for Badger, who was a keen sailor, they allowed him to go to a ship school, which is how he ended up on the *Tobermory*. He felt this was by far the best thing that had ever happened to him.

Badger was the first person Ben met when he joined the ship, and it was Badger who showed him round. Ben liked the other boy's sense of humour, and his kindness too. It was important to be kind to other people, Ben thought, and Badger was always kind. He was also rather good at doing things, although he never boasted about any of the things he could do.

Then there was Thomas Seagrape, who came from Jamaica, where his mother was the captain of a small ship. Thomas was one of those people whom every-body liked the moment they met him, as they realised that he was the sort who

Thomas Seagrape

Poppy

would never let them down. And they were right: Thomas always did what he said he would do. If he promised to help you with something, he would be there when it had to be done. People appreciated that.

He and Ben also saw things the same way. They laughed at the same jokes, liked the same food, and sometimes even felt as if they were brothers. That is always a good test of a friend: would you like your friend to be your brother or your sister? If the answer is yes, then that means that you have found a really good friend.

Fee's closest friend on board was probably a tall red-haired girl called Poppy Taggart. Poppy came from a sheep farm near Alice Springs, right in the middle of Australia. She had never been to sea when she first came to the *Tobermory*, but she had always wanted to be a sailor. Since their farm was so far from anywhere, Poppy's parents decided that because she had to go off to boarding school anyway, they might as well send her all the way to Scotland, where the *Tobermory* was based.

"That was one of the best choices they ever made,"

said Poppy, who loved being on the *Tobermory* – as everybody did.

Fee shared a cabin with Poppy, and so they saw a lot of each other. But she had other good friends on board, in particular Tanya Herring and Angela Singh. Tanya had been a

Tanya Herring

stowaway, which is somebody who hides on a ship and is only discovered on board once the ship has left harbour. She had run off to sea after her mother died because she had been sent to live with a cruel aunt and uncle who made her work in their dog kennels. Although Tanya's father was still alive, he was always at sea and Tanya had no way to contact him except through her awful aunt and uncle. But she hoped that one day their paths would cross. Fortunately, she was allowed to stay on the *Tobermory* when she was discovered, as she had been very helpful in nursing the Captain's dog, Henry, when he had broken a leg.

Angela Singh was a bit timid at times, but was discovering her courage and hoped one day to be as brave as the rest of them. Fee liked her because she was always happy to help in the background. Some people are a bit pushy and always want to be in charge of what is going on. Angela was not like that

Angela Singh

at all, and Fee valued that quality in her friend.

So there they were, a band of friends, all at school together on the *Tobermory*, which was now heading back to port – a place that was also called Tobermory, which is the main town on the Scottish island of Mull. As the ship came closer to shore, people began to talk about their plans for the coming school holidays.

"I'm going to have to stay on board," said Badger, rather sadly. "My Mom and Dad have sent me a message. They're having some important meetings and think it would be better for me to stay on the ship rather than come home."

Ben frowned. From what he had heard of Badger's parents, this was typical of them. They were always far too busy to pay much attention to their son, who would have loved to see more of them if only they could have found some time for him in their over-full schedules. "Won't you feel lonely?" he asked. "After all, the holidays are two whole weeks, and that's a long time to be by yourself."

Badger shrugged. "It might be a bit quiet," he said. "But I'm not going to be all by myself, you know.

Poppy isn't going all the way to Australia just for two weeks, and then there's Tanya, who hasn't really got a home to go to. There will be three of us still on board. And of course there'll be Henry – he stays on board."

"And what about Thomas?" asked Fee. "Will he go all the way back to Jamaica?"

"He's going to stay with an aunt in London," replied Badger. "He's all right. He told me that she's a great cook, and makes just the right sort of spicy Jamaican food he likes. He says he has a great time with her and his cousins."

Poppy had been down below, but now she arrived on deck, along with Tanya.

"What are you talking about?" Poppy asked.

"The school holidays," Badger replied. "I was telling Ben and Fee that I'll be staying on board, and that so will you and Tanya."

"That's right," agreed Poppy. "We can keep one another company."

Ben drew Fee aside. "Listen," he whispered. "Can't we ask them to come home with us?"

Fee sucked in her cheeks. She always did that, Ben noticed, when she was thinking hard.

"Well?" he prompted.

Fee's cheeks returned to normal. "What will *they* say?"

Ben knew that when Fee referred to *they* she was speaking about their parents. She had always called them *they* or *them.*

"We could ask them," he said.

"But they'll still be at sea, won't they?"

Ben looked at his watch. For his last birthday he had been given a special nautical watch that displayed all sorts of information, including the movement of tides and the depth of water – which was very useful when diving. This watch also showed what day of the month it was, and this enabled him to work out where his parents' submarine would be.

"They'll be off the coast of Ireland by now," he said. "They'll be making their way back to Scotland. They were going to pick us up in Tobermory at the end of term – which is tomorrow, isn't it?"

Fee had an idea. "We could radio them," she suggested. "We could ask Mr Rigger if we could use the radio room."

Ben thought this was a good idea, but he pointed out that there was something else they had to do before they tried to contact their parents. "We need to ask Badger and the others if they want to come with us. You can't just assume that they would."

"Well then," said Fee. "Let's do that."

Ben and Fee had been having this conversation in whispers – now they turned back to their friends.

"We've had an idea," announced Ben. He nudged Fee. "You ask them, Fee."

Fee drew in her breath. "You don't have to say yes,"

she began. "If you want to say no, then just say it — we won't be offended."

Poppy looked puzzled. "Ask us what?"

"Yes," said Badger. "What's the big question?"

"We — that is, Ben and I ..." Fee began.

"Come on," encouraged Poppy. "Get to the point!"

"All right," said Fee. "The question is this: would you — and by that I mean you, Poppy, you, Badger, and you, Tanya — would you all like to come and stay with us during the holidays?"

"Rather than staying on board," added Ben.

Poppy's eyes opened wide. "You mean it?" she asked.

"Of course," said Fee.

Poppy did not hesitate. "Then the answer's *yes*. And thanks a million!"

"Me too," said Badger. "I'd like to accept."

"And I would too," said Tanya. "I'd love to come."

"Then we can ask our parents," said Ben. "I'll go and speak to Mr Rigger about using the radio room."

Mr Rigger taught seamanship — the art of sailing, of staying afloat and of not sinking. He was a kind man with a very famous moustache, one of the best-known moustaches at sea. This moustache would twirl around in the breeze, providing a reliable way of telling which direction the wind was coming from. This is something that sailors need to know, so that they can trim their sails to get the best possible push

Mr Rigger

from the wind.

He was also in charge of the radio room, and gave lessons on how to work the radio. So when Ben asked if he could try to contact his parents, Mr Rigger suggested that the others should come along so it could be a radio lesson as well.

The radio room was Ben's favourite part of the ship. He loved the look of the equipment – the dials and lights, the switches and buttons. He watched carefully as Mr Rigger stood by the equipment; behind him were Poppy, Badger, Tanya and Fee, also watching intently.

"Right," said Mr Rigger from behind Ben's shoulder. "You turn it on by flicking that switch over there. You do it, Ben."

Ben did as he was told, and immediately lights were illuminated on the radio's front panel. Ben had memorised the frequency of his parents' radio, and he now twirled one of the dials so that it was in exactly the right place.

Mr Rigger was impressed. "Pretty good, so far," he said. "Now start your transmission."

Ben took a deep breath. He had read about how

you should talk when using a radio, but it was not always easy to remember. Leaning forward, he said into the microphone, "Calling *Seabed Explorer*, calling *Seabed Explorer*." *Seabed Explorer* was the name of his parents' submarine; with any luck they would be on the surface and able to hear the call, or, if they were below, they would have their special underwater aerial out.

Mr Rigger smiled. "Not so good, Ben."

Ben blushed, trying to work out where he had gone wrong.

Mr Rigger looked at the others. "Anybody see the mistake he's making?"

Fee held up a hand.

"Yes, Fee?" said Mr Rigger.

"He hasn't pressed the *transmit* button," she said, looking reproachfully at her brother.

Ben looked down at the floor. She was right: he had forgotten the most elementary thing you have to do when using a radio. It was a very bad mistake.

"That's right," said Mr Rigger. "And he also forgot to say who he is. You must *always* say who you are. Always." He turned to Ben. "Try again, Ben."

Badger glanced sympathetically in Ben's direction. Everybody could make mistakes, he thought, and he wanted to point that out to Fee. But now was not the time.

This time Ben pressed the transmit button so

firmly that he almost broke it.

"Careful," said Mr Rigger.

Ben began to speak. "*Seabed Explorer*," he said. "*Seabed Explorer. Seabed Explorer.* This is *Tobermory, Tobermory.* Over."

"Good," said Mr Rigger. "Always remember to say *over* so that the other person knows it's his or her turn to speak."

There was silence. Very faintly, a crackle of static – the sort of noise made when you crumple a paper bag – came through the speaker. And then, still faint but clear enough, there came an answering voice.

"*Tobermory, Tobermory, Tobermory,*" the voice said. "This is submarine *Seabed Explorer, Seabed Explorer.* Receiving you loud and clear. Over."

Fee was excited. "That's my mum!" she exclaimed.

Ben then spoke again, explaining about their three friends being left on board during the holidays and asking whether they could come home with them. After he had finished, there was a pause at the other end. "Please say yes," whispered Fee, although her mother could not hear her.

The radio crackled into life again. "*Tobermory, Tobermory,*" said Mrs MacTavish. "Of course they can come. We'll collect all five of you tomorrow in Tobermory." And then, to bring the exchange to an end, she said, "Out."

Ben was about to say goodbye when he was

stopped by Mr Rigger. "Never speak after the other person has said *out*. *Out* means the end. It means *goodbye, so long, farewell, au revoir, hasta la vista*. Don't say anything after somebody's said *out*."

Ben nodded. He looked at Badger, who was smiling at him. Then he looked at Poppy and Tanya – and they were both smiling too.

"We're going to have a great time," said Ben.

"That's fine," said Mr Rigger. "But remember it's just for two weeks. Then you're back here and we set off for the Caribbean. You're going to learn a lot over there, you know. There are very strong winds, ideal for sailing. And the islands are very interesting too. There'll be lots to do."

Ben nodded. They were looking forward to the trip, especially Thomas Seagrape, who came from Jamaica, and had been telling them all about how warm the water was there, and how blue, and how delicious the feeling of sand between your toes on the long beaches was. Going home for the holidays with their friends would be fun – but the Caribbean, thought Ben, would be even greater fun. He could barely wait.

The end of term was marked the next day by a speech by the Captain on the top deck in front of the whole school and the *Tobermory* teachers. The Captain's speeches were never all that long, and he always said much the same thing, but that day he was roundly cheered by everyone, such was the electric atmosphere of excitement.

"You've all earned your holiday," said Captain Macbeth. "After three months of hard work and tough sailing you're entitled to have a bit of a break. Don't forget, though, what you've learned this term, and above all, remember to be kind to the landlubbers!"

This brought a laugh. Landlubbers were the people who never went to sea – people who went to ordinary schools on dry land.

The Captain then presented a few prizes to people who had done particularly well. There was a prize for Bartholomew Fitzhardy, who was generally regarded as the most skilful sailor on the entire ship. He was a popular member of the school who had spent part of the last term in the sick bay, recovering from a nasty case of infectious boils, and everybody cheered as he received his prize, a large book on navigation. Then there was the star navigation prize for Amanda Birtwhistle, a member of Middle Deck – where Ben and Fee had their cabins. Amanda was astonishingly good at telling the ship's position from the stars, and this was the third time she had received this award – and she deserved it.

But the prize that brought the biggest cheer was the one awarded to Tanya. Her prize was the Admiral

Amanda was astonishingly good at
telling the ship's position from the stars ...

Nelson Prize, which was always given to the person who had done the kindest deed that term. Tanya was awarded that for helping to treat Henry's broken leg, and most people felt she richly deserved the prize.

But not everybody thought this. Three members of the school scowled when Tanya walked forward to receive the prize, and one of them actually hissed under his breath – not that the Captain heard. The leader of this little group was William Edward Hardtack, the unpopular Head Prefect of Upper Deck, and his two equally unpleasant friends were Geoffrey Shark, widely known for his cruel ways and his hairstyle, which was remarkably similar to the fin of a shark, and Maximilian Flubber, whose ears moved whenever he told a lie – which was often enough. These three mocked anybody who won a prize, although it was widely believed that they would love to win a prize themselves.

William Edward Hardtack

"There should be a prize for awfulness," Poppy said. "And we all know who'd get that one – William Edward Hardtack."

Hardtack, who was standing nearby, over-heard this. "I heard you, Carrot-Top," he

16

Maximilian Flubber

hissed. "I'm going to get you one of these days. You just watch out."

Calling Poppy Carrot-Top because of her red hair was typical of Hardtack, who always tried to think of a cutting nickname for people. It did not worry Poppy, of course, who just laughed it off, but there were some who were upset by such insults.

And there were also those who would be frightened by Hardtack's threat to 'get' them. He was always threatening to 'get' people. Poppy was quite capable of looking after herself, but it could be different for people who felt a bit more vulnerable.

After the Captain had finished, the liberty boats – the small rowing boats used to get ashore – were lowered to take everybody from the *Tobermory* to the town of Tobermory itself, where the ship anchored for the holiday. There people would be taken on

Geoffrey Shark

17

two large buses that would cross to the mainland of Scotland by ferry before making their way to the station at Fort William, where they would either be picked up by their parents or board a train that would eventually get them home.

Once everybody had gone, there were only the teachers and Ben and Fee's group of friends left on board. The five students stood at the gangway, their kitbags ready beside them, waiting for the arrival of the *Seabed Explorer*.

"I hope they haven't forgotten us," said Fee nervously.

"Of course they haven't," Ben reassured her. "They've never let us down before, Fee."

They did not have to wait too long. About half an hour after everybody else had gone ashore, Poppy cried out that she had seen something moving in the sea not far from where the *Tobermory* was anchored.

Rushing to join her at the railing, the others gazed where Poppy was pointing. Was that commotion in the water just a bigger wave, or perhaps a playful seal, or was it something else? It *was* something else. Slowly a dark shape rose under the water and then, with a final thrust, it broke the surface, its conning tower throwing off the water in a cascade of foam.

"That's them!" shouted Ben. "That's our sub-marine!"

They made their way over to the sub-marine in

Cook

the rubber boat that Ben and Fee had brought with them when they first joined the *Tobermory*. It was a bit of a tight fit for the five of them and their kit-bags, but they managed to squeeze in, and the calm water that morning made the crossing quite easy. As they climbed onto the submarine, they waved to Matron, who was standing on the deck of the *Tobermory* with Cook, her husband.

"Have a good holiday," shouted Matron across the water.

"We will," shouted back Poppy, who was good at projecting her voice across wide spaces. She had learned to do that in the Outback in Australia, she had explained once. "When there's nothing about you for miles and miles," she said, "you learn

Matron

19

to shout. None of us really bothers with telephones in the Outback – we just shout. People usually hear you."

Ben and Fee's mother welcomed them all aboard and helped them lower their kitbags down the conning tower ladder. Then, when they were all safely on board and the rubber dinghy had been deflated and stowed away, they were shown the bunks where they would sleep on the journey to Glasgow. This trip would take more than a whole day, as research submarines are not designed to go all that fast, and there would be fish and other marine life to look at on the way. Once in Glasgow, the submarine would be tied up in dock and they would all go off for the two weeks of the holiday in the small village where Ben and Fee's family had their home.

Fee introduced the three guests to her parents, and everybody shook hands.

"We're delighted that you can spend your holiday with us," said Ben's father. "We've heard a lot about you in the postcards that Ben and Fee have been sending home."

Mrs MacTavish looked at her watch. "Well, if everybody's ready," she said, "I think we should go. I don't know if you've had breakfast already, but I was planning to serve fried eggs once we were underway."

Ben glanced guiltily at Fee. Cook had made a good breakfast for everybody that morning, but he always liked his mother's fried eggs and he was anxious for his friends to try them.

"Even if you've already eaten I see no reason why you shouldn't have two breakfasts," said Mr MacTavish. "If you have a second breakfast you can eat the things you forgot to eat at the first."

There was no arguing with that, and the submarine hatch was closed. Then, amid a thick mass of bubbles, the vessel began to sink below the surface. At the observation window, the three guests – Poppy, Tanya and Badger – watched in fascination as the *Seabed Explorer* began to glide through the water. It was all so different down below. Large fish swam past, unconcerned by what they thought was just another sea creature – a whale perhaps; fronds of seaweed swayed gracefully in the water like tree branches in the wind; even crabs could be seen scuttling about sideways on the sea bed below.

After half an hour, Mrs MacTavish served fried eggs. These were every bit as delicious as they smelled, and everybody wolfed them down. Then they were all given a turn at steering the submarine, while Fee explained the controls to them. They would not stay underwater for the entire trip, she explained, as it was quicker to travel on the surface like any other boat.

They made good progress, and by late afternoon they were level with the top of the island of Jura, a small mountainous island off the Scottish coast. And that was where something alarming occurred. It was the sort of thing that makes you feel cold inside when you remember it later on. It was the sort of thing that makes you wake up at night in a cold sweat, just thinking about it. And like many such things, it all took place rather quickly and without anybody being prepared for it. This is what happened.

CHAPTER 2

The whirlpool

Just off the west coast of Scotland there is a channel of water that is not very wide called the Gulf of Corryvreckan. It is far too broad, though, to swim across – unless you're a very strong long-distance swimmer. And even then, trying to swim across the Gulf of Corryvreckan would be a very foolhardy thing to do. The reason for that is because in the middle of this channel is the third largest whirlpool in the world.

Fee told Poppy and Tanya all about it as they made their way down the coast of Scotland in the MacTavish submarine.

"A whirlpool?" marvelled Tanya. "A real whirlpool? With water that goes round and round like this?"

She made a circling movement with her hand, and Fee nodded.

"Yes," Fee said. "You know what it's like when you take the plug out of the bath and the last of the water is draining away, it goes round and round faster.

That's a small whirlpool. It's the same thing."

"But where's the sea draining to?" asked Poppy. "You're not saying there's a plug, are you?"

Fee laughed. "No. There's no plug. What happens is this. When the tide comes in it wants to get through the narrow channel, you see. But in the middle of the channel there's a sort of underwater mountain. It doesn't reach the surface, but it's pretty big."

Poppy thought she could see what was coming. "So when the tide comes in it has to go round the mountain?"

"That's exactly what happens," said Fee.

"And when water goes round and round," said Tanya, "you always get a sort of hole in the surface – just like in the bath."

Fee nodded, and went on to explain that the whirlpool in the sea only happened when the tide was strong. Once the tide stopped coming in or going out – at a point called slack tide, when the water wasn't going anywhere – then the sea could be as calm as a sheet of glass.

"So it's safe to go through then?" asked Poppy.

"Perfectly safe," answered Fee. "All you have to do is work out when slack tide is, and start going through then."

Tanya shivered. "I'm not sure I could work that out," she said. "And what if you got it wrong?"

"If you got it wrong," said Fee, "you'd be in trouble. Your boat could be sucked down and then …"

"Then that's the end of your boat," said Poppy. And added, as if in an afterthought, "And of you too!"

Tanya brightened; she had thought of something. "Of course, if you're in a submarine – as we are – then it wouldn't matter, would it? You would get sucked down, but that's fine in a submarine, which is meant to be underwater."

Fee thought for a moment. "No, Tanya, you wouldn't be all right," she said. "If you were sucked down in a submarine you could be dashed against the underwater mountain." She imagined what would happen then. "Or you'd be forced down onto the sea bed. If either of those things happened, your submarine could get a hole in it, and if you get a hole in a submarine …"

"You never come up again," finished Poppy.

"So the important thing," said Tanya thoughtfully, "is not to make a mistake."

It was at this point that Mr MacTavish came into the cabin where the girls were having this chat.

"Time for you to go on watch, Fee," he said. "Your friends can come and help you. I'll go and tell the boys that you're going to relieve them." Ben and Badger had been on duty steering the submarine, and now it was their turn to have a rest while the girls took over.

On their way to the control room, Mr MacTavish reminded Fee that they were approaching the Gulf of Corryvreckan.

"You know about the whirlpool, don't you?" he asked. "You know we can only go through on slack tide?"

Fee told him she did. "I'm going to check the tide tables," she said. "Then, if necessary, we can wait further out at sea until the tide is right and we're ready to go through."

"That's exactly what to do," said her father. "You're obviously learning a lot on that school ship of yours."

He was right. They had all been learning about tides with Mr Rigger. He had explained in a seamanship class one day how the tide spent six hours coming in and then the next six hours going out. That made four tides every day: two high and two low.

"Except in some places," Mr Rigger said.

Poppy's hand went up. "Yes, in parts of Australia," she said. "Where I come from."

"That's right," said Mr Rigger. "In northern and southern Australia you only get …"

" … one of each a day," provided Poppy. "One high and one low. That's because we've got two oceans around us – the Pacific and the Indian."

"And they cancel each other out a bit," said Mr

Rigger. "Tides are just like water slopping round in a bowl – it bumps into things and gets all mixed up."

Fee remembered this as she went to the locker in the control room to find the tide tables. It would be easier to work things out before they took over from the boys, so she and Poppy began to page through the tables. These set out exactly when high and low tides would be on any particular day. They were quite simple, and she had used them before in Mr Rigger's class.

But then Fee made her mistake – and it was a mistake that could have cost them all their lives. The timings of tides differ widely depending on where you are. So if you are in the south of England, the time of high tide there might be very different from the time of high tide in the north of Scotland. Or if you are on the coast of Maine, say, high tide may not be at the same time as down at the tip of Florida.

But that does not make tide tables for one place useless for others. You can still use the tables – all you have to do is adjust the times. Fee forgot to do this. And as a result, when she said that slack tide would be at two o'clock that afternoon, she was wrong. At two o'clock the tide would be coming in, and the water would be racing through the Gulf of Corryvreckan. So if they started to go through the channel at two, then they would be heading straight into danger.

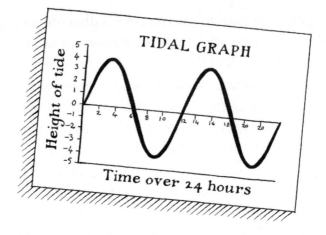

TIDAL GRAPH

Height of tide

Time over 24 hours

"We'll go through at two o'clock," she said, when she assumed control of the submarine.

"Have you checked the tide tables?" asked Mr MacTavish.

"Yes," said Fee. "We've just done that."

"Good," he said. "Then we'll be safe."

He was wrong.

They went through submerged, as it is always calmer down below the waves than on the surface. At first the submarine moved slowly as it glided through the dim green water, but then, quite suddenly, it began to rock slightly.

It was Tanya who noticed it. "Why are we moving up and down?" she asked.

"Are we?" asked Fee. She had not felt anything unusual, but then Poppy agreed with Tanya. She, too, could feel an unusual movement – rather like being on an aeroplane when it flies into some bumpy air, she thought.

Now the rocking sensation became much stronger, and Fee noticed it too. Peering through the observation glass, she tried to work out what was happening. It was hard to make anything out, as the light, falling from the surface above in eerie shafts, was very weak. She thought she could see something ahead – a dark shape rising up from the seabed, but the next moment it seemed to have disappeared. Deciding to be on the safe side, she swung the submarine to the right – to starboard, as she had been taught to say. The nose of the underwater craft shifted, but not very much, and the next moment it swung back, as if pushed by some great unseen hand.

"Is something wrong?" asked Poppy, a note of anxiety rising in her voice.

"I'm not sure," said Fee.

"We're going faster," said Tanya. "And look, I think we're being turned round."

The submarine was now beginning to go out of control. As firmly as Fee pushed on the control column, equally – or even more – firmly did it resist. Outside, visible through the observation window, there were bubbles and pieces of seaweed being flung about as if they were trapped in an enormous washing machine.

Fee's parents had been alerted to the fact that something was wrong when they felt the unusual movement, and they were now trying to get back into the control room. But every time they took a step forward, they were thrown back by a lurch of the vessel. It was impossible for them to help.

As the submarine spun round the great stack of rock Fee racked her brains to think of what she should do. She had tried steering the submarine, but it was simply not responding. And that was no surprise, with that force of water rushing round it, hurling it in a desperate circle.

She closed her eyes for a moment and thought, *What would Mr Rigger do?* As she did so, she thought she saw him, standing there in his fine white uniform, his moustache waving in the breeze. And then she remembered something he had once said: *If all else fails, try putting the ship in reverse!*

She opened her eyes again. They were very close to the rock now, and she thought that at any moment they would hit it. And then, reaching forward, she pulled the lever that would put the submarine's engine into reverse.

For a moment nothing happened. But after a few seconds, as the powerful engine went into reverse, she felt the vessel slow down. This gave her the chance to turn the control column as far over to starboard as it would go.

Poppy, too, could feel an unusual movement – rather like being on an aeroplane when it flies into some bumpy air.

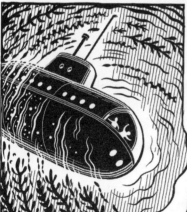

The submarine was now beginning to go out of control ... Outside, there were bubbles and pieces of seaweed being flung about as if they were trapped in an enormous washing machine.

And then Fee remembered something Mr Rigger had once said: *If all else fails, try putting the ship in reverse!*

"We're turning," shouted Poppy.

Fee pushed harder, and suddenly, as a cork or a float might pop out of the water when released, they shot out of the whirlpool into calmer water.

"You've done it!" yelled Tanya, flinging her arms round Fee. "You've done it, Fee!"

Poppy gave a whoop of delight. "I thought we wouldn't make it," she said.

Now that the submarine was steady once more, Fee's parents were able to join her in the control room. They were followed by Ben and Badger, both boys having been knocked about a bit by the violent bucking of the submarine.

With Mrs MacTavish now at the controls, the others gathered round the chart table to discuss what had gone wrong. As soon as she saw her tide calculations on a scrap of paper, Fee realised what her mistake had been.

"It was my fault," she said miserably. She found herself shaking as she spoke; it was only now dawning on her what a close-run thing it had been.

Mr MacTavish put an arm about her shoulder. "Every single one of us," he said, "has made a bad mistake some time or other." He paused, and looked at the others about him. "Hands up anybody who's never made a mistake."

Not a single hand went up.

"Well, there you are," he continued. "So nobody's

blaming you, Fee. The important thing at sea – and anywhere else, I suppose – is to learn from your mistakes."

Fee felt grateful to her father. She would have understood had he told her off publicly in front of her friends for threatening the safety of the submarine – and risking the lives of all of them, for that matter – but he did not. He was a kind man, and she was proud to have him as her father.

"Thank you," she whispered under her breath.

He smiled. "I bet you won't make that mistake again!" he whispered back.

"I won't!" she promised.

The rest of the trip went smoothly, and early the next morning the submarine slipped safely into its berth in Glasgow. All hands went on deck to help tie it to the posts on the edge of the quay and after that it was time to offload everybody's kit and begin the journey to the MacTavishes' house. This they did in a hired minibus, large enough to fit them all in, and soon they drew up in front of an old and rather ramshackle house on the edge of a small country town.

"Here we are," announced Mr MacTavish with a smile. "MacTavish Headquarters. Ben and Fee will show you all to your accommodation."

There were only three bedrooms in the MacTavish house: one for the parents and one for each of the twins. These were large bedrooms, though, as is often the case in older houses, and so it was easy to convert them to a girls' dormitory for Fee, Poppy and Tanya, and a boys' dormitory for Ben and Badger. There would certainly be enough room for everybody, but what about beds?

That problem was easily solved, as all three guests had brought their hammocks from the *Tobermory*.

"You can tie one end of your hammock to that clothes-hook," explained Ben to Badger, "and the other to the cupboard door. You'll be fine."

In the girls' dormitory, two hammocks had to be slung, but there were more hooks in that room, and so there was no problem with that.

"Everybody's fixed up now," said Fee to her mother. "The hammocks are up and the kit-bags are unpacked."

"Good," said Mrs MacTavish. "I think it's time for some more fried eggs."

As they sat about the large kitchen table, fried eggs were served together with a good helping of baked beans. There were also large bowls of Scottish oatmeal porridge and a slice of chocolate cake to finish. It was a magnificent meal, and everybody felt very full and content at the end of it.

"I've got a feeling we're going to have a great time here," remarked Badger as they sat playing cards in the sitting room after the meal.

"I think so too," said Poppy.

Tanya felt the same. "And so do I," she echoed.

Although nobody knew it, they were in for a nasty surprise the next day. One that none of them could have foreseen, and one that was going to make them all – and Tanya in particular – extremely scared.

In the storm drain

After breakfast Mrs MacTavish asked Ben and Fee to go into the town centre to buy supplies.

"We need bread and milk," she said. Then, remembering other things, she added, "And some butter too. Jam. Breakfast cereal. And … oh yes, and potatoes."

Fee wrote it all down in her notebook. All the students on the *Tobermory* had been taught to carry a notebook with them at all times; this was useful for jotting down things like duty rotas or timetables, or new nautical words that they might need to look up. So when somebody shouted out things like, "Haul in the starboard sheets!" they would write down 'sheets' and find out later on what the word meant. (It did not mean the sort of sheets you have on a bed, as there were no beds on the *Tobermory*, just hammocks. Sheets, they soon found out, were a special sort of rope.)

Fee looked up from her notebook. "And chocolate?"

Mrs MacTavish hesitated. She knew her daughter had a weakness for chocolate, and she knew that it was not a good idea to eat too much of it, but then a little of the things you like never harms anybody. And so she said, "All right, chocolate too, but not too much, Fee – I know you when it comes to chocolate!" Badger smiled, but said nothing. Chocolate was his weakness too.

All the friends went into town, making the short journey on foot, carrying bags in which to bring the shopping back to the house. Fee and Ben were well-known in the shops, and were greeted cheerfully by the shopkeepers, who all knew about the *Tobermory* and were eager to find out how they were getting on at their new school.

They were in the last of the shops, buying the chocolate, when Fee suddenly broke off from what she was saying.

"I think we'll have six bars of that one over …" She trailed off.

"Which one, Fee?" asked the shopkeeper.

But Fee did not hear the question. She had noticed there was something wrong with Tanya, who had suddenly stiffened, and then drawn back, her hand coming up to cover her face.

Poppy had seen this too. "Tanya?" she asked. "Are you all right?"

Tanya's response was to move sharply, so that she

was standing behind Poppy, sheltered from anybody who might look into the shop through the wide plate-glass window.

Now Badger became concerned. "There's something wrong," he whispered. "Tanya's had a terrible fright."

Ben looked puzzled. What could possibly have had this dramatic effect on Tanya? One moment she had been fine, chatting away with the rest of them, and then the next it was as if she had seen a ghost. *Perhaps she has*, he said to himself. *Perhaps that's just what she's seen.* But then he noticed her peering through her fingers, and he saw that she was looking out into the street. He followed her gaze. There must be something out there that was frightening her: but what was it?

It did not take him long to work out what it was. Parked directly outside the shop was an old car, and seated in the front were a man and a woman, both wearing hats. The man had a brown hat with a floppy brim; the woman had a fancy, rather pointless hat – all feathers and ribbons. It was not a hat that served any useful purpose – it wouldn't provide any protection from the sun, and if it rained it wouldn't be long before it was reduced to a sodden mess.

But it was not the hats that really attracted Ben's attention – it was the faces beneath them. There was only one word for them, he said to himself, and that word was *dangerous*. In fact, had he thought about it a bit longer, he would have realised there was more than one word that suited them: *evil, mean,* and *dishonest* were just as good. Of course, the way people look does not always reflect the way they really are, but there was something about this pair that made Ben think appearances were not deceptive.

Fee was soon at Tanya's side.

"Tanya," she said. "What is it?"

Still shielding her face, Tanya replied in not much more than a whisper. "Those people outside," she said. "Them – do you see them?"

"Yes," said Fee. "We've all seen them. What about them?"

"It's my uncle and aunt," said Tanya in a voice strangled by fear and emotion. "It's them!"

Fee drew in her breath. She remembered the story that Tanya had told her of how she had been sent to live with relatives who cared little for her and who made her work for nothing in their dog boarding kennels. She remembered how Tanya had eventually run away and reached Mull, where she had stowed away on the *Tobermory*.

Fee beckoned the others over and told them what Tanya had just said.

Ben glanced out of the window. "They're still there," he said. "They're showing no signs of moving."

"Do you think they've seen you, Tanya?" asked Poppy.

"I'm not sure," replied Tanya. "I can't really tell."

"I don't think they have," said Badger. "It looks to me as if they're just waiting."

"What are we going to do?" asked Fee. "We can't stay in here forever."

Poppy decided to take control. She was the oldest member of the group, so she was the natural leader. She had also always been good at getting out of dangerous situations, such as when she had found herself once in a sleeping bag with a snake. That had been a tricky situation: the snake had slithered into her sleeping bag when she was on a school camping trip. Snakes sometimes do that because they like the warmth. Of course, if you rolled over or moved in your sleeping bag too suddenly there might be serious consequences.

Poppy had done the right thing. Snakes like warmth, but they don't like to be too warm, so Poppy had told her friends simply to take down the tent, thus allowing the sun to shine directly on her sleeping bag. Under the Australian sun, a sleeping bag quickly becomes an oven, and the snake, feeling the heat, decided it was time to slither out again. That had been hard for Poppy, as she had been obliged to lie quite still as the snake slid slowly over her body, then – and this was the hardest part – over her face. She would never forget the sight of its small dark eyes and flickering tongue as it moved its sinuous body over her. Nor would she forget the words of the expedition leader afterwards when he told her what sort of snake it had been. "That was a taipan, Poppy," he had said. "Not the best snake to have in your sleeping bag! In fact, one of the worst. One bite from that and … well, let's not think about that."

The situation they now found themselves in was bad, but not as bad as that. *And*, thought Poppy, *if I can deal with a taipan, surely I can deal with Tanya's uncle and aunt.*

A plan came into her mind. "Right," she said, addressing Ben and Badger. "This is what we do. We're in here, right?"

Ben and Badger nodded.

"And they're out there," Poppy continued.

Again Ben and Badger nodded.

"So what we need to do is to get Tanya out without their seeing her."

"Sure," said Badger. "But how do we do that? It's broad daylight and they're sitting in their car right outside. If anybody comes out of this shop they'll see."

"Only if they're looking," said Poppy quickly. "What we need is a diversion."

"To make them look at something else?" asked Fee.

"Exactly," said Poppy. "So …"

She began to explain her plan. "Ben," she said, "you and Badger should go out first. Cross the road, and then, when you're on the other side, start having an argument. Start shouting."

Ben looked at Badger, and Badger looked back at him. They were both puzzled.

"Then," went on Poppy, "start a fight."

"A real one?" asked Ben.

"No," replied Poppy. "But make it look real. Don't hurt each other, but start pushing and kicking. And all the time keep shouting so that …"

It dawned on them all at the same time.

"So that their attention is attracted," said Badger.

"And they'll be looking over there, while back here …" added Ben.

"… Tanya creeps out with Poppy and me," finished Fee.

"You've got it," said Poppy. And then, following what they had all been taught on the *Tobermory* about briefings, she went on to add: "Any questions?"

Everyone thought the plan was perfectly clear, so they began to put it into action.

"Ready, Badger?" asked Poppy. "Ready, Ben?"

Badger and Ben looked at one another. They were the best of friends, and it was difficult for them to imagine having an argument, let alone actually fighting.

"What shall we fight over?" asked Ben.

Badger thought hard. He had never hit anybody – as far as he could remember – and it was difficult to think of a reason to do so now. "Let's imagine we're in one of those old western movies," he said. "One cowboy comes into the saloon and says, 'You stole my cattle!' Then they begin to throw punches – you know the sort of thing."

Ben tried not to laugh. "All right," he said. "Let's try that."

Ben and Badger felt the eyes of the man and the woman in the car follow them as they left the shop and started to cross the road. Now was the time for them to begin their argument, and they did so by giving each other a preliminary push. This led to shouting.

"Watch where you're going!" shouted Badger, loud enough, he hoped, for the people in the car to hear.

"You watch where *you're* going!" Ben shouted back.

Now they were on the opposite side of the road and they were aware that the people in the car were still watching them. But they were also aware that in the background Poppy had opened the door of the shop and behind her, ready to come out, were Tanya and Fee.

"Now," whispered Badger. "We'd better start right now."

Ben glanced towards the car. "Right," he whispered. "You first."

43

Badger shook a fist at his friend. "You stole my cattle!" he shouted.

Ben was taken completely by surprise. The absurdity of what they were doing suddenly came home to him. *You stole my cattle!* How ridiculous. And then, completely unable to control himself, he started to laugh.

"That's not what you're meant to do," hissed Badger. "Look mean. Look angry."

"I can't," gasped Ben between fits of laughter. "How could I steal non-existent cattle?"

This had an unexpected effect on Badger, who started to laugh as well.

"My cattle!" he shouted. "Where have you hidden them?"

Ben found this even more amusing, and was now bent double with laughter. Try as he might, he could not stop himself – it was all so ridiculous.

Over on the other side of the road, Poppy was wondering what was going on. The boys had been told to have a stage fight, not to fall about with laughter. What had gone wrong? But then, when she looked at the car, she saw that the plan was working. The man and woman were both clearly surprised by what was happening and were themselves starting to laugh. Laughter, as we all know, can be infectious. If one person starts to giggle, then soon everybody can find themselves doing the same thing.

"Now!" whispered Poppy to Tanya and Fee. "Let's go right now."

They stepped out on to the pavement and began to walk away, quickly but, they hoped, not so quickly as to attract attention.

It worked. As the two people in the car stared at the sight of Ben and Badger doubled up with uncontrollable laughter, the girls made their way down the street and turned the corner to safety. A few minutes later, they were joined by Ben and Badger, who had by now only just managed to stop laughing.

"What happened to you two?" demanded Poppy. "What was so funny?"

Fee joined in the accusation. "You could have ruined everything," she said. "You were meant to have a fight, not to fool around."

"I'm sorry," said Badger. "We just couldn't help it. You know how it is when you try not to laugh – it gets harder and harder until eventually you lose control."

Tanya did not want the boys to feel guilty. "The important thing is that it worked," she said. "You distracted them for long enough. We got away unnoticed, and that's what counts."

"But what do we do now?" asked Fee. "We can't go back to pick up our shopping with them still around."

While Poppy was thinking how to answer, they

heard the sound of a car engine revving. Ben looked up and saw that the car in which Tanya's aunt and uncle had been sitting was now coming round the corner at high speed straight towards them. Without wasting a moment, he pushed Tanya against a wall while he and Ben stood in front of her. To anybody passing they would have looked just like a group of young people huddled together talking about something.

It was their best chance, thought Ben, and it worked. As the speeding car drew near, he got a glimpse of the driver and his passenger hunched in their seats, their eyes fixed intently on the road in front of them. But then, just as the car drew level, the woman turned in her seat and looked straight at them.

And at that precise moment Tanya, anxious to see what was happening, moved to one side of Ben and Badger. She was only exposed for a moment, but it was enough. She had been seen. With a screeching of brakes, the car came to an abrupt halt.

Poppy realised what had happened and reacted quickly. "Follow me," she said. "We're going to run for it."

They did not need any further encouragement. Taking to their heels, the group of friends followed Poppy as she dashed down a path that joined the roadside not far from where they had been standing, their legs pumping away as fast as they could.

For some distance the path ran alongside some gardens. Not far off, though, the houses gave way to countryside, with fields, and, in the distance, a large wood. Poppy hesitated; she was unsure whether to continue that way and so risk being exposed, or whether they should go over a fence and into one of the gardens. She looked behind her, and saw in the distance the man running after them, waving his hands and shouting something she could not make out.

There was no time to consider other possibilities – Poppy knew that she had to act, and quickly. Looking around, she spotted a smaller path that led off between two gardens. She could not see where it went, but if they followed it they would be out of sight of their pursuer, at least for a minute or two.

She made up her mind. "Turn here," she shouted as she swerved off.

They followed her – Ben, Badger, Tanya and Fee – all of them beginning to feel the exhaustion that comes with pushing your limbs to the limit. As Poppy had suspected, they could not be seen from the path they had just left, and this gave them a precious opportunity to hide. But where? The new path had a low fence on each side, but even if they jumped or clambered over either one, there was not enough cover in the gardens to hide five people.

It was Fee who saw it. "Look!" she shouted to Poppy, and pointed to the ditch that opened up off one side of the path. "There's our chance."

Poppy looked, and immediately saw what Fee meant. The ditch very quickly became deeper, and at the end of it was the gaping round entrance of a storm drain.

"Down there," Poppy shouted, pointing to the mouth of the drain.

One by one they scrambled into the ditch, and one by one they crawled into the drain's dark mouth. If they had not been so frightened, it would have been a difficult task, but fear can make things much easier. In no time at all they were inside, crawling forward into the darkness, led by Poppy, with Ben bringing up the rear.

"I think that's far enough," said Poppy, her voice amplified in the cramped space. "He's not going to find us here."

Ben glanced over his shoulder. They were now some distance away from the entrance to the drain, which was a round circle of light behind him.

"Is everyone all right?" asked Poppy.

They all replied that they were fine, although every one of them had their own unique fears. Ben was worried about spiders. A place like this was an ideal place for them to build their nests, he thought, and they would not take kindly to people clambering

48

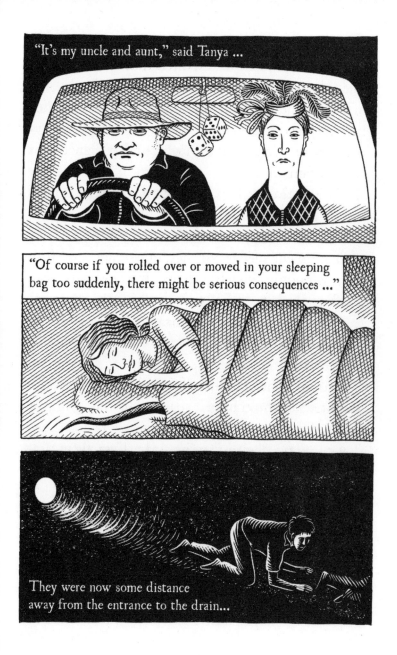

all over them. Badger felt generally uneasy; he did not like tightly enclosed places, and this made his skin come out in goose bumps. Tanya was frightened of the dark, and wished she had brought a torch with her. Fee was wondering about rats. She had always been scared of rats, and the thought that there might be hundreds of them in the storm drain made her shiver. And Poppy was worried that the roof might suddenly collapse, burying them all alive.

But nobody spoke of any of these fears, so there was complete silence. Silence in the dark is worse than silence in the light, because the mind can imagine all sorts of things. And the dark also seems to slow down time, making one minute seem like ten.

It was after only a couple of these very long minutes that they heard a sound outside. Ben turned – in so far as he could turn in that cramped space – and looked behind him.

There was a pair of legs. Somebody had climbed down into the ditch and was standing directly outside the mouth of the drain.

Then there was a man's voice, which said, "They went this way. I'm pretty sure they went in here."

From somewhere not far away a woman could be heard. "Are you sure? I think we've lost them, the little devils. Let's get back to the car."

Further down the drain, sandwiched between Poppy and Badger, Tanya shivered in fear. She had recognised the voices as being those of her uncle and aunt.

"All right," said the man. "Let's go."

In the darkness, Poppy nudged Tanya. "You're going to be all right," she whispered. "They're leaving. We'll be able to crawl out in a moment or two."

Tanya believed her. But in doing so, she, like the others, was falling for one of the oldest tricks. If you are hiding from somebody and you can hear but not see them, never *ever* come out of your hiding place if you hear them say they're about to go. Just don't. The reason for this is that they are probably only saying this to lure you out. Then, when you do come out, thinking that all is clear, there they are, waiting for you …

And that is exactly what happened. After a couple of minutes, Poppy announced to the others that it would be safe to crawl back out of the drain. She did not bother to lower her voice, as she imagined there was no longer any threat.

She was wrong. Immediately after they emerged into the open and were busy dusting themselves off, they heard a shout.

"Ha!" yelled a voice. "So you thought we'd gone away, did you? Well, we've got a surprise for you!"

For a moment everybody froze. The man and the woman were not far away, and it was clear that there was not much time to act. Poppy, though, made her decision quickly. Grabbing hold of Tanya, she pushed her back down to the entrance of the drain.

"Quickly!" she shouted. "Crawl in again. I'll come with you."

Tanya did as she was told, and by the time the man and woman reached the ditch again, both girls had disappeared. The man was furious.

"Come out of there, Tanya!" he roared. "Come out immediately!"

The others – Ben, Badger and Fee – stood by. There was nothing they could do – the man was large and strong-looking, and the woman had brightly painted red fingernails that looked as if they could deliver a good scratch.

"Come out or I'll come in and get you!" shouted the man.

When no reply came from the drain, he took off his coat and passed it to the woman. "Hold this," he said. "I'm going to have to drag her out myself."

Getting down on his hands and knees, he began to squeeze into the narrow mouth of the storm drain. Ben's heart sank as he saw this – there would be no escape now for Tanya, he thought: she would be dragged out and taken away by her dreadful uncle and aunt.

But then, just as Ben was about to give up hope, the most extraordinary thing happened. Tanya's uncle was too fat for the space, and no sooner had he worked half of his bulk into the mouth of the drain than he found himself stuck. He kicked his legs and wiggled his hips, but his very fat middle was the problem. It was firmly lodged in the entrance and there seemed to be no way of shifting it.

"Pull me out!" he shouted.

His wife leaned down to grab his legs. She gave a tug, and then another tug, but this seemed only to wedge him in more firmly.

"Harder!" shouted the trapped man. "Pull harder!"

It was very difficult for Ben and the others not to laugh. He knew that you shouldn't really laugh at the misfortune of others, but there was something richly comic in seeing this unpleasant man trapped in this way.

"Don't just stand there," snapped the woman, "help me!"

"Why should we do that?" asked Badger.

"Because ..." shouted the woman. "Because ..."

But whatever she was about to say would not have been heard because at that moment they heard a shout. Looking up, Ben saw that a good distance away Poppy and Tanya had emerged from the other end of the drain and were waving at them.

"Quick," muttered Badger. "Let's go."

Fee looked down at the stuck man and his increasingly angry wife. "But what about them?" she asked.

"She can go and get help," said Ben. "There are

plenty of houses nearby. Someone'll help drag him out."

The decision made, Ben, Fee and Badger ran as fast as they could to join Poppy and Tanya. Then, wasting no time, the whole group made their way home, leaving their pursuers to wait for rescue.

"Anything happen this morning?" asked Mr MacTavish at lunchtime.

Ben looked at Badger and Fee looked at Poppy. Tanya looked up at the ceiling.

"Not much," said Ben.

Then he began to laugh, and the others soon joined in.

"I don't see what's so funny," said Mr MacTavish.

"Well it wasn't really funny," said Ben. "It was scary. But it ended well."

"What ended well?" asked Mrs MacTavish.

"We were chased," said Ben. "And we ended up in a storm drain. Then this man who was chasing us got stuck in the entrance. He couldn't move because he was too fat."

Mr MacTavish laughed. "Really, Ben," he said. "You have the most active imagination. Do you expect me to believe that?"

"And the shopping?" asked Mrs MacTavish. "What happened to the shopping?"

"Oh," said Poppy. "Yes, the shopping. Well …"

"We had to leave it behind," said Fee. "When you're being chased down storm drains it's easy to forget all about shopping."

Mr MacTavish gave his daughter a strange look. "How every odd," he said. "But I suppose you were all having fun."

How lucky is that?

During the rest of the holiday the five friends were careful about when they went out – and where. In fact, they spent a great deal of the time in the house or in the garden rather than risk being spotted again by Tanya's uncle and aunt.

"I wish we could go somewhere," said Fee. "I'm getting fed up staying in all the time."

Ben knew how she felt, but he was sure that they were doing the right thing in lying low for the rest of their holiday. "It's just not worth the risk," he said. "We have to think of Tanya."

Fee nodded. "Yes," she said. "We have to stick by her."

Of course, they found things to do. There were plenty of board games in the house and Badger very much enjoyed those. Poppy was keener on playing cards, and she soon taught them all the rules of canasta. There was also a very complicated Chinese game called *mah jong*, involving small bricks with highly coloured pictures on them. Both Ben and Fee had been taught how to play this, and they now explained the game to the others. Soon they were playing the game with all the enthusiasm of experts, and the hours sped past.

Eventually the time came to return to the *Tobermory*.

"We'll miss you," said Mrs MacTavish. "The house is going to seem very quiet."

"You can come to stay any time you like," said Mr MacTavish to Badger, Poppy and Tanya. "Our door is always open."

Badger, Poppy and Tanya all said how grateful they were for the holiday. Then, their kit-bags packed for the new term, the five friends were driven to the railway station, the first leg of their journey back to the School Ship *Tobermory*.

Arriving back on board, they were greeted by the familiar sight of Mr Rigger standing on the deck, checking their names off against a list.

"MacTavish, B.," he said, "welcome back. Mac-Tavish, F., welcome back. Tomkins, welcome back. And Taggart and Herring," he said, referring to Badger, Poppy and Tanya, "There you are, too – welcome back to the *Tobermory*."

Ben and Fee took their kit-bags to their cabins and stowed their gear. It was much easier this time than at the beginning of the previous term, as they knew exactly where things should go. Then it was up to the sick bay, where they were asked whether they had suffered from any coughs or sneezes while they were away.

"We can't be too careful about coughs and sneezes," said Matron. "Bring one cough or sneeze back on board and before you know it the whole ship will go down with coughs and sneezes. Look what happened with Bartholomew Fitzhardy. If we hadn't isolated him, the whole ship would have had infectious boils."

At dinner that night, with the whole school assembled in the dining hall, Captain Macbeth spoke about what lay ahead.

Captain Macbeth

"Now listen to me," he began. "I hope you've all had a good break and are ready for the new term. Is everybody looking forward to it?"

The whole school answered with one voice. "Yes, sir!"

"Good," continued the Captain. "There's going to be a lot to do because, as you know, we're going to be making a long voyage. That will mean a lot of hard work. Is everybody ready for hard work?"

Again there came a swelling chorus of "Yes, sir!"

But was everyone so enthusiastic? Absolutely everybody? Not quite, because if you had looked at the Upper Deck table, sitting there at the end of it, in their usual places, were the three well-known troublemakers, William Edward Hardtack, Geoffrey Shark and Maximilian Flubber. Their lips moved at the same time as everyone else's, but they were not saying *Yes, sir!* Far from it. Hardtack was actually saying, *You wish!* Shark was saying, *That'll be the day!* And Flubber was saying, *Give us a break!*

But Captain Macbeth saw and heard none of this as he continued with his speech. "This term our destination is the Caribbean Sea. As you all know, this is the sea that lies off the southern part of North America, just above the top of South America. It is full of islands, some of which you will have heard of and others whose names might not be so well-known. We shall be sailing from the top of the Caribbean to the bottom, and will be visiting some of these interesting islands."

There was a murmur of excitement at this news.

"Yes," said the Captain. "It's going to be an interesting trip, especially for those of you who like swimming in warm blue water ..."

This brought a cheer, and an enthusiastic bark from Henry, who was wagging his tail enthusiastically at the Captain's side.

"… that's so clear you can see the sand below and the fish as they swim past …"

There was another cheer at this.

"And for those who like coconuts …"

Loud cheering.

"And steel bands …"

More loud cheering.

"And beaches with more shells than you can imagine possible." Prolonged clapping and cheering.

Once the Captain had finished his address, dinner was served. Cook had outdone himself and had prepared a fine meal of fish served with fried potatoes, buttered pumpkin and spicy beans. For dessert, he had made a traditional naval pudding, stuffed with currants and served with vanilla custard. It was one of the best meals ever eaten on the *Tobermory*.

It was while they were on the way out of the mess hall that Badger fell. He was walking alongside Ben, discussing what they would be doing the next day, when he suddenly stumbled. As he went down, Ben tried to break his friend's fall, but was too late. Bending down, he helped Badger to his feet.

"Are you all right?" he asked anxiously.

"I think so," replied Badger, gingerly trying the

weight on his right foot. But then he gave a yelp of pain and almost fell to the ground once more. Had Ben not been there to support him, he would have fallen hard.

"I'll help you get to the sick bay," said Ben. "Put your arm round my shoulder and I'll support you."

Slowly they made their way down the corridor towards the sick bay. As they did so, Ben asked Badger what had happened.

"I was pushed," muttered Badger. "Didn't you see?"

"Pushed?" asked Ben. "Who pushed you?"

"I swear it was Shark," said Badger. "He was walking past me when it happened. I remember seeing him out of the corner of my eye and then suddenly I felt pressure in my ribs, as if somebody was pushing me. I'm sure it was him."

"Report him," said Ben. "He can't be allowed to get away with it."

Badger shook his head. "What's the point? There are no witnesses, and he'll simply deny it."

Ben knew that his friend was right. The first rule of people like Hardtack, Shark and Flubber was never to be seen doing anything. *If nobody saw me do it, then I didn't do it* – that was their motto.

Matron was in the sick bay when they knocked on the door. She was alarmed to see Badger being supported by Ben and immediately took the injured boy's other arm and helped him to a seat.

"Now, what on earth have you been doing?" she asked. "And on the first day of term too!"

"It wasn't his fault, Matron," blurted out Ben. "He was pushed by …"

Badger gave Ben a warning look, and his voice trailed off as a result.

"Out with it," snapped Matron. "Who pushed him?"

Badger winced. "I think it was Geoffrey Shark," he said. "But I can't be sure.'

"I suppose nobody saw it happen," said Matron.

"No, they didn't," said Badger.

Matron sighed. "It's always the same old story," she said. "Nobody sees anything. Those boys know they can get away with whatever they want to because they're confident that nobody will ever say anything." She fixed Badger with a reproachful stare. "I'm sorry you didn't trust me enough to tell me straightaway," she said.

For a few moments Badger forgot about the pain in his ankle. He *did* trust Matron, and it seemed to him unfair for her to accuse him of not trusting her. "I'm telling the truth," he said heatedly. "Nobody saw what happened. There really isn't anyone who can back me up."

Matron looked at him. She was a fair-minded person and she was also a good judge of character. She knew Badger was not the sort to tell lies.

"I'm sorry, Badger," she said. "I shouldn't have doubted you. It's just that I've become so fed up with people not seeing anything when something nasty happens. But I shouldn't have spoken to you in the way I did."

Badger cheered up. "That's okay, Matron," he said. "Don't worry about it."

Matron now began to examine his ankle. Badger grimaced as her fingers found the painful bits.

"I think you've pulled a ligament," said Matron. "Sometimes, if you put muscles and what-not under strain they don't like it too much." She smiled. "You'll live, Badger! But I'll rub some of my ointment on it and then wrap the ankle in a bandage. You'll be as right as rain in no time at all."

Badger was pleased to hear that Matron would be using her ointment. This was based on a secret recipe she had devised that was known to nobody else other than Cook, who prepared it for her in one of his kitchen pots.

When applied to a sore arm or leg, the skin would tingle. This feeling would last for several minutes while the ointment did its work. Then, in almost all cases, the pain of the original injury would disappear.

People said that Matron could have made a fortune if only she and Cook had bothered to make larger quantities of it to sell. But she just laughed at such suggestions. "I don't want to be rich," she said.

"I'm happy doing exactly what I'm doing – being matron on the *Tobermory*. And Cook's happy too, being cook on board. There's more to life than money, you know."

As Matron rubbed her ointment into his ankle, Badger closed his eyes and counted to one hundred. By the time he reached seventy-five, the pain was almost gone, and by the time he came to one hundred his ankle felt entirely normal.

"There you are, young Badger," said Matron, as she finished bandaging his ankle. "Keep the bandage on for two days. You're excused climbing in the rigging, physical training, and anything involving running. I'll write a note to Mr Rigger to that effect."

She gave Badger the note and he and Ben left her cabin. It was only half an hour or so until lights out, and the two boys decided to go to the recreation room to see if they could find Thomas Seagrape. They had not seen him since they returned to the ship and they were keen to find out how his holiday had gone.

Thomas was not in the recreation room – in fact the only people there were the Hardtack gang.

"So it's you, Striped One," sneered Hardtack. This was his nickname for Badger – badgers being striped – and although it was not in the slightest bit funny, Hardtack and his friends thought it very witty.

Badger did not reply. This clearly enraged

Hardtack, who rose to his feet and said menacingly, "I was addressing you, Tomkins. Something wrong with your ears?"

Badger glanced at Ben, who could tell that he was uneasy.

"I've got nothing to say to you, Hardtack," Badger said evenly.

This only seemed to make things even worse. Hardtack was now on his feet and was advancing towards Badger in a menacing way. "You been talking to Matron?" he said, in a voice full of threat. "You been telling her stories?"

Badger remained calm. "It's my own business what I do," he said calmly.

Hardtack was now right up against him. Grabbing the front of Badger's shirt, he pulled him towards him, almost lifting him off his feet in the process. "You see, O Striped One," he hissed, "me and the boys here definitely do not approve of people who go running off to Matron every time they trip over their own shoe-laces, do we, Geoffrey? Do we, Maxie Boy?"

Shark shook his head, his famous shark's fin quiff wobbling to underline his message. "We definitely don't approve of such behaviour, Tacky. No, we don't like it one little bit."

Tacky, thought Badger. What a suitable name for somebody called Hardtack. It made him sound ... well, so tacky.

Badger answered truthfully. "I went to see Matron about my ankle. Somebody pushed me after dinner."

Hardtack looked at him scornfully. "Oh, poor you! A sore ankle! Let's take a look at it and see if we can help." As he spoke, he grabbed Badger's jacket and shook him. Badger struggled, but the bully's grip was too firm.

He bent down and at that moment Badger saw his chance. Using his knee, he pushed Hardtack away from him as hard as he could. Hardtack had not been expecting this and lost his balance almost immediately. "Watch out!" he shouted, as if in warning to himself, before toppling over and falling flat on his face.

Seeing their leader go down, Shark and Flubber rushed forward to help him. This gave Ben and Badger the chance to run for the door and slam it behind them. It was then they noticed that someone had left the key in the lock. Doors are almost never locked on board a ship, but now, on impulse, Badger turned the key.

"We can't lock them in," Ben said.

Badger grinned at his friend. "Why not? They started it. And it'll keep them from bothering anybody else for a while."

Ben still looked doubtful.

"Somebody will hear them and let them out," said Badger. "They won't be in there for long."

Ignoring the sound of frantic banging on the door, the two friends returned to their cabin to get ready for lights-out. Badger grinned with pleasure as he recalled the look on Hardtack's face as he had tumbled to the ground. Whatever had happened, Badger had been acting in self-defence, and everybody knows you are entitled to protect yourself if somebody like Hardtack attacks you.

After lights-out, lying in their hammocks, the two boys spoke across the room to each other.

"What do you think's happened to them?" asked Ben.

"Oh, they'll be out by now," said Badger. "Mr Rigger always checks up on the recreation room before lights out. He'll have heard them banging on the door."

"Serves them right," said Ben in a tired voice.

Badger did not reply, as he had already dropped off to sleep. But Ben knew he would have agreed had he been awake. That's the nice thing about having a good friend: you always know what he or she would say, even if they are fast asleep at the time and unable to say anything at all. Badger was his good friend, and he would always stand by him. *I'm lucky*, he thought, as he felt sleep overcome him. *I'm lucky to be here on this ship, with my good friend Badger, and a voyage to the Caribbean starting the very next day. How lucky is that?*

CHAPTER 5

On Captain's parade

The departure of a big ship from harbour always involves a lot of hustle and bustle. The next morning the *Tobermory* was due to sail two hours after morning muster. That muster – which is a gathering of the crew on deck – was at six o'clock, just a short time after everybody had got out of their hammocks, washed their faces and climbed into their sailing clothes. Now, standing in long lines on the well-scrubbed deck, seagulls shrieking and dipping above their heads, the whole crew stood to attention as Mr Rigger inspected their turn-out. Up and down the lines he walked, stopping occasionally to check that a buckle was fitted correctly or to pass some comment on the creases in a uniform.

'Smart turn-out," he muttered to Thomas Seagrape as he looked him up and down. "Good work, Seagrape."

Standing in front of Tanya, he looked closely at her belt. "Good standard, Herring," he said. "But the belt needs a bit more polish, I think."

Next to Tanya was Henry, who was sitting to attention, his coat neatly brushed and his leather collar polished with brown boot-polish.

"Good dog, Henry," said Mr Rigger. "Very smartly turned-out," he added, as Henry wagged his tail in appreciation.

He moved on, and had now reached Badger and Ben, who were standing next to one another. Mr Rigger paused, looked quickly at Badger's uniform, and then said rather sharply, "Captain's Parade, Tomkins. Immediately after we set sail. Understand?"

Badger swallowed hard. Captain's Parade involved reporting to the Captain's cabin when you had done something wrong. And it was not just any simple misdemeanour that would get you on Captain's Parade – it had to be a serious offence.

Mr Rigger now moved on to Ben. "Same for you, MacTavish, B.," he said. "Captain's Parade. Don't be late!"

Ben felt miserable. "What have we done?" he whispered to Badger after Mr Rigger had moved on.

Badger was good at talking without moving his lips. "It'll be that business with Hardtack and Co.," he said from the side of his mouth.

"But they started it," protested Ben.

"They won't have said that," replied Badger. "They'll have given a very different story.'

The inspection came to an end and they all took up their stations. Ben and Badger were on anchor duty, along with Thomas, Poppy, and Tanya.

"What did Mr Rigger have to say?" asked Poppy. "I saw him talking to you."

"We're on Captain's Parade," said Ben.

Poppy made a sympathetic face. "Oh dear," she said. "What did you do?'

Badger answered her question. "We defended ourselves," he said. "That's all.'

"Then you'll have nothing to worry about," said Tanya. "Captain Macbeth is always fair."

They did not have time to talk about it any longer, as the order had come to raise the anchor. This was supervised by Miss Worsfold, who was in charge of geography and anchoring. She told them how to switch on the large windlass that would haul up the great anchor, and then how to control the lowering of the chain into the anchor locker.

"Watch your fingers!" she shouted. "Don't take your eyes off the chain for a moment."

They were very careful. Thomas had told them of a man who worked in his mother's boat in Jamaica, and who had let himself be distracted while bringing up the anchor one day and had caught a thumb in the windlass. "That was the last he saw of his thumb," said Thomas. "So I'm going to be extra careful."

Poppy shuddered. "So am I," she said. *You have to*

be careful when you're working, she thought, remembering a man on her farm, back in Australia. He was an expert in sheering sheep and had often won competitions to find the fastest sheep-shearer in the country. He was a tall man with a great black beard, and on one occasion, when he let his concentration slip, he had shaved off his own beard as well as the sheep's fleece – all in the space of fifteen seconds. It was a new record, people said, and had never been equalled since.

With the anchor up and stowed, they watched as the people working on the sails hauled on the halyards – the special ropes that ran the sails up the masts. Then the sheets were brought in and the sails trimmed to fit the wind. Like a dog kept back on the leash and then released, the *Tobermory* leapt forward, its prow cutting cleanly into the waves, the spray from its bows whipping past in a spume of white. Over on the port side the coast of Mull slipped past, while ahead of them the broad Atlantic opened up. They were on their way. Thousands of miles of empty ocean lay ahead.

"I can't believe it," Ben said to Badger. "We're on our way to the Caribbean!"

Badger smiled. "Yes, it's quite a thought," he said.

But then his smile faded. He remembered that they were both on Captain's Parade, and it was now time to report down below.

"We'd better go," he said to Ben. "We'll only get into more trouble if we're late."

Mr Rigger was waiting for them outside the Captain's cabin. After telling the two boys to wait outside, he knocked on the door and went in. Ben looked at Badger. He had always thought of Badger as being braver than he was, but now he thought his friend looked every bit as anxious as he himself felt.

The door opened and Mr Rigger gestured for them to follow him back inside. There was Captain Macbeth sitting at his desk, his arms folded, looking as severe as they had ever seen him.

"Tomkins and MacTavish, B.," announced Mr Rigger.

The two boys stood to attention in front of the desk, their arms straight down their sides, looking – and feeling – as uncomfortable as it is possible to be.

"Now then," began Captain Macbeth. "You know why you're here, don't you?"

Ben looked at Badger.

"We had a fight with Hardtack," said Badger. "He started it, sir …"

The Captain cut him short. "I'm not talking about what went on before," he snapped. "I'm talking about your having locked Hardtack, Shark and Flubber in the recreation room. Did you do that or did you not?'

Badger nodded. "Yes, sir, we did, but you see,

Hardtack grabbed me and ..."

Again the Captain interrupted him. "Listen, Tomkins, what you need to know is that on board ship the most important thing is safety – you know that, don't you? We've told you about it a hundred times if we've told you once.'

"Yes, sir," said Badger. "But ..."

"No buts," said the Captain. "And locking somebody in a cabin or any other place on board ship is very, very dangerous. It's one of the worst things you can do." He paused. "Do you know why?"

Now he transferred his gaze to Ben. "Well, MacTavish, maybe you know the answer to that?"

Ben thought quickly. Why was it so dangerous to lock a door on board ship? And the answer came to him immediately. If anything happened – if the ship should start to sink or be swamped by a giant wave – anybody locked in a cabin or somewhere else would be trapped and could drown. That was the reason – and it was a very good reason too. He imagined just how terrifying it must be to be in a locked cabin, tilting at an angle, with the water rising around your ankles ...

He explained all this to the captain, who nodded his approval.

"Exactly," he said. "So you know how dangerous it is, and yet you boys did it. You locked those three in the recreation room and they were there until Mr Rigger heard them banging on the door later."

"They were locked up for a good half-hour, Captain," said Mr Rigger, casting a disapproving glance at Badger and Ben.

"If anything had happened during that time," the Captain went on, "those three boys would have been in great danger."

For a short while they stood in silence as the Captain's words sank in. Then Badger offered his apology. "We're very sorry, Captain," he said. "We didn't think."

"You didn't think," repeated the Captain. "No, you didn't, did you?"

Ben decided it was time for him to say something too. "I'm sorry as well," he said. "I know it was stupid, but we didn't realise just how stupid it was at the time."

"Well, at least you have the grace to admit it," said the Captain. He glanced at Mr Rigger. "And I dare say you boys were provoked. You know what provoked means?"

Ben wasn't entirely sure.

"It means that they made you so cross you did something back to them," said Captain Macbeth. "In other words, they asked for it."

Ben thought this was exactly what had happened. "Yes, sir, they provoked us."

Captain Macbeth now noticed the bandage on Badger's ankle. "What happened to your foot, Tomkins?" he asked.

Before Badger could reply, Ben gave the answer. "Geoffrey Shark pushed him," he said.

The Captain looked thoughtful. "It seems to me that you boys should keep out of the way of that group," he said. "Just don't cross them."

"But they're always looking for trouble," protested Ben.

"Well then, one of these days they'll probably find more trouble than they bargained for," said the Captain. "But in the meantime just keep out of their way."

The Captain sighed. "I'm going to have to punish you, you know. I don't particularly want to do it, but I can't let a very foolish act like that go unpunished." He paused, looking at Ben and Badger as if he felt extreme disappointment.

"I shall take into account that you didn't start the whole business," he continued. "So rather than a whole week of cleaning the heads, you're to have three days. Make a note of that, Mr Rigger."

Ben caught his breath. Cleaning the heads – the toilets – was the most unpleasant job on the ship and he had to do it for three whole days. It was the worst thing that had happened to him for a long, long time. And Badger felt the same. He kept his eyes fixed on the floor, but Ben could tell that he was every bit as upset as he was.

"Now, boys," said Mr Rigger. "You've heard what

your punishment is to be. So you may as well start. Do an hour of cleaning now and one in the evening after dinner. The same goes for tomorrow and the day after – three days, as you heard the Captain say."

Mr Rigger led them out of the Captain's cabin. Once outside, he leant down and whispered to them. "All right, I'm sorry that it's come to this. I know you were sorely provoked, and I personally don't blame you for what you did. But the Captain's right, you know – you can't risk life on board a ship. So just go off and do your cleaning. It's only for three days."

Ben and Badger went off to fetch the brushes, mops and buckets they would need for their task. Neither spoke. Both felt ashamed and angry: ashamed that the whole school would know of their punishment and angry that the world could be so unfair. If anybody deserved to be cleaning the heads it was Hardtack, but that, it seemed, was never likely to happen.

It was not easy work. The floors had to be washed with seawater and scrubbed until any vestiges of dirt were removed. Then the walls had to be wiped from floor to ceiling and the taps on all the basins polished until they shone like silver. Then the toilets themselves had to be hosed down, given a good cleaning with round-headed brushes and then doused in disinfectant strong enough to make your eyes water.

Ben and Badger only had to clean the boys' heads, but even so it took them a full hour to complete the task. And then, just as they were preparing to pack away all the cleaning equipment, Maximilian Flubber came in.

"Oh," he said, pretending to be surprised to see them, even though by now the whole school had heard about the punishment. "So you're on cleaning duty. Bad luck!"

Badger and Ben both ignored him and continued to put the equipment away. But what happened next could not be ignored, for Flubber, suddenly making a retching sound, shouted out. "Oh my goodness, I'm going to be sick! Oh no, how awful! Sea-sickness! My poor stomach!"

And with that, he brought up his half-digested breakfast all over the floor Ben and Badger had so painstakingly cleaned.

The two boys watched in horror. It would have been perfectly possible for Flubber to reach one of the toilet bowls or even one of the basins and be sick there. That would have been much easier to deal with. But no, he simply brought it up all over the floor.

"So sorry," said Flubber, wiping his mouth with his sleeve. "I hope you don't mind too much cleaning it all up."

From just outside they heard laughter, and saw

"That was the last he saw of his thumb," said Thomas. "So I'm going to be extra careful."

"... he had shaved off his own beard as well as the sheep's fleece – all in the space of fifteen seconds. It was a new record, people said, and had never been equalled since."

"Oh my goodness, I'm going to be sick! Oh no, how awful! Sea-sickness! My poor stomach!"

Geoffery Shark and William Edward Hardtack peering round the half-open door.

"Feeling better, Max?" asked Shark. "Far better to get it out of the system, you know!"

"Much better, thanks, Geoff," Flubber replied. "Pretty nasty stuff, though, sick. Still, the cleaners are still on duty, so they'll take care of everything."

And with that, Flubber left the heads and joined his two sniggering friends in the corridor. Ben looked at Badger in despair. "Do we have to?" he asked.

Badger nodded. "I suppose we do," he said.

They set to their unpleasant task and it was a full half-hour before they managed to remove the last trace of Flubber's breakfast. Their cleaning duties over, they took a hot shower, using as much soap as they could lay their hands on.

"Two more days of this," moaned Ben. "And it's all Hardtack's fault."

"Oh well," said Badger. "Let's try to think of something nice instead. That sometimes works, you know. If you have something horrible to do, think of something good and it takes your mind off it."

"Such as?" asked Ben.

Badger thought for a moment. "The Caribbean," said Badger. "Beaches of white sand. Palm trees. Coconuts."

"Coconuts!" exclaimed Ben.

"Yes," said Badger. "Aren't they delicious?"

"I can't wait," said Ben.

They went on deck. The coast of Mull had now vanished, and the swell of the sea was becoming more pronounced. This was the real Atlantic now. The heaving of the sea out here had the force of a full ocean behind it; the wind, unrestrained by land, had a whole sky at its back. As they went to stand at the railing and look out into the open sea, they started to forget their unpleasant experiences down below. Both of them felt they were at the beginning of some great adventure. And so it turned out, though neither would never have guessed just how exciting – and dangerous – that adventure would be.

CHAPTER 6

A wind from Africa

It would take three weeks for the *Tobermory* to sail across the Atlantic. If they had been able to go in a straight line it would have been quicker, but sailing ships have to follow the winds. And winds don't always move in the direction you want them to, nor blow as strongly as you may like.

"We're making good progress," announced Mr Rigger after they had been at sea for four or five days. "You'll see that our course is taking us down towards the Azores, which are islands right out in the Atlantic. Once we get down there we'll pick up a wind from Africa that'll blow us straight across to the Caribbean."

A wind from Africa! Fee loved the sound of that; she had always wanted to see Africa, and although it was out of sight over the horizon, at least they would feel a wind that came from there. She imagined that it would be a warm wind, with a bit of sand in it, perhaps, carried all the way from the great Sahara

Desert. Or it might smell of West African jungle, a green sort of smell, a reminder of the tall trees and hanging vines it had caressed before it set out to sea.

Fee liked to think about such things, but for the most part everybody was kept far too busy to daydream. Not only were there all the usual school classes – history and science, and things like that – but there were lessons devoted to subjects associated with the sea. One of these was a class run by Miss Worsfold on the sea and its creatures which was very popular and always packed.

The first of these classes was about dolphins. Just about everybody had seen dolphins by now, as these friendly creatures appeared almost every day, frolicking in the bow wave, accompanying the ship across mile after mile of sea before suddenly losing interest and darting off on some other business.

Miss Worsfold

"They probably like the sound a ship makes," said Miss Worsfold. "They like the creaking sound of the timbers. Perhaps it sounds like music to them."

The class on dolphins was followed by one on whales.

"Whales have songs," explained Miss Worsfold. "They sing these to each other over hundreds of miles. They sound like random squeaks to us, but the whales know what they mean."

They learned about how people used to hunt whales for their oil, and how some cruel people still did that.

"They are very intelligent creatures," said Miss Worsfold. "They have feelings, just like us."

Tanya, in particular, was saddened by the story of the whales. She thought of the men in their whaling ships, with their sharp harpoons, chasing these gentle creatures until they were too exhausted to flee any more. "How would they like it," she asked Fee, "if they were to be chased by whales with harpoons?"

Then there was a lesson on squid – odd, rubbery creatures with long tentacles and great dish-shaped eyes. Many squid are not all that big, Miss Worsfold told them, before going on to talk about giant squid, which live far below the surface and whose tentacles can be much longer than a person.

"They're very elusive creatures," Miss Worsfold explained, "so we don't see them very much. But they are there, nonetheless, lurking way down below where the light never penetrates and it's dark and gloomy."

Poppy glanced at Tanya, and shivered. "Imagine having a giant squid down below you when you're swimming," she whispered.

Tanya closed her eyes. "I'd never get in the water if I thought there might be a giant squid beneath me."

"But how would you *know*?" asked Poppy. "We can't see much underwater, can we? So there could be giant squid anywhere, just waiting for their chance."

"To do what?" asked Tanya, by now thoroughly alarmed.

"To shoot up from down below and grab you in its tentacles," said Poppy.

"Now, girls," said Miss Worsfold. "Don't worry about things that are very unlikely to happen. There have been no recorded instances of a giant squid attacking anybody."

"There's always a first time," muttered Poppy. "We knew somebody back in Australia who said that dingoes – those wild dogs we have – never harmed anybody. Then he went for a walk in the bush and he never came back. They just found his shoes – that was all."

"Eaten by dingoes?" asked Tanya.

"Who knows?" said Poppy.

About a week into the voyage the wind that had blown them down from Scotland disappeared. Mr Rigger was sure that the wind from Africa would not be long in coming, but for a few days they were becalmed, the sails hanging limp on their spars or fluttering gently and ineffectually from their masts like washing hung out to dry.

Mr Rigger explained that they could turn on the engine, but that this would use a lot of fuel.

"We like to save our fuel," he announced to the school at morning muster. "There may come a time when we really need it to get out of trouble. So the Captain says we're to wait this out. The wind will come sooner or later, and that'll set us off on our course like a rabbit across a field."

Being becalmed was a strange sensation. The sea was utterly still – a great flat expanse of water, like silvery glass, reflecting the sky. Every so often, the surface would be broken by movement of some sort – a flying fish, perhaps, escaping from a bigger fish below – but for the most part it seemed as if the ocean was one great sleepy pool.

The *Tobermory* drifted with the current, but even that was not very strong, hardly moving in places, and sometimes seeming just to go round in circles. Since they could make no progress in their voyage, the Captain authorised swimming parties, with each deck being allowed to take it in turns to have a dip from the side of the ship. A special ladder was lowered with a platform at the end of it where people could sit and dangle their legs in the water or use it to dive from.

Ben and Fee were both strong swimmers, as were Poppy and Badger. Thomas was even better, as he had been brought up in Jamaica in a house right beside the sea, and he had been able to swim ever since he had been old enough to walk. Tanya and Angela Singh were not so experienced though, and Angela in particular was nervous about entering the water.

"Come on!" shouted Poppy from the water when it was Middle Deck's turn to swim alongside the gently drifting ship. "The water's really warm."

Standing on the platform, Tanya and Angela hesitated. They looked at each other for encouragement.

"Shall we?" asked Tanya.

"I suppose so," said Angela. "We don't want them to think we're scared."

They looked at the others, who were already frolicking in the sea. Ben had dive-bombed Badger, who was energetically splashing him in self-defence. Poppy and Thomas were busy checking how far they could see underwater – not far, as it happened, as the ocean was very deep at that point and everything disappeared into an infinite blue beneath them.

At last Tanya jumped in, quickly followed by Angela. When they resurfaced, both were smiling. The water was pleasantly warm – just as Poppy had said it would be – and it was a wonderful feeling to be surrounded by such a vast amount of ocean. It was like floating in space, with nothing below you …

Below you … Tanya began to think about what might be down there. Thousands of feet of water, and … Suddenly she was gripped by a feeling of cold panic. Giant squid … what if a giant squid were at this very moment looking up from the depths with its eyes as big as saucepans, gazing at legs dangling down from above? And what would a giant squid think in such circumstances, especially if it happened to be hungry?

It was too much to bear, and Tanya struck out for the side of the ship as fast as she possibly could, creating a splash of white water as she did so. Shaking with fear, she hauled herself up onto the platform, noticing, as she did so, that Angela was not far behind her.

"I suddenly felt really frightened," Tanya said to Angela as she helped her friend out of the water.

"Me too," said Angela. "Giant …"

"… squid," completed Tanya.

They looked at one another and smiled. They didn't care if people laughed at them; better to be thought scared than to be wrapped in the tentacles of a giant squid.

Tanya and Angela soon dried off and climbed the ladder back onto the main deck. They were still in their swimming costumes and were about to go down below to change when they sensed the first breath of wind.

"Did you feel that?" asked Tanya. "I'm sure I felt a breeze."

Angela nodded. "Yes," she said. "That was definitely a puff of wind."

Within a few seconds, there could be no doubt about it. What had started as the tiniest breath, the smallest movement in the air, now became a gust of real wind, hot and dry. It was the wind from Africa.

From his position on the quarter deck, Mr Rigger walked swiftly over to the railing. Putting his whistle to his mouth he blew several long blasts – the agreed signal to let the swimmers know they had to come in immediately. In the water down below, Poppy looked up and waved to show that she had heard the whistle.

"Time to get out," she called to Fee, who was floating in the water a few yards away.

Fee looked around. Ben, Badger and Thomas had not climbed out yet and must still somewhere in the water nearby – but where?

"Have you seen the boys?" she called to Poppy.

Poppy had not. "They'll have heard the signal," she said. "They'll turn up. Maybe they're on the other side of the ship."

She was right – at least about their being on the other side of the ship. But she was wrong about their having heard the signal. When Mr Rigger blew his whistle, Ben, Badger and Thomas had been diving underwater, seeing how long they could hold their breath, and they were quite unaware that it was time to get out. And now, even as Fee and Poppy clambered out of the water onto the platform, the *Tobermory* began to move through the water. Although her sails were not yet even half-full, they were beginning to billow in the wind, providing some pull for the ship.

Down in the water, Badger tried to keep calm.

"Try not to panic," he called out to his fellow swimmers. "Save your strength to keep afloat."

"Do you think they've seen us?" spluttered Ben.

"I hope so," said Thomas. "Otherwise …"

Ben felt himself gripped by despair. He felt terribly lonely – a tiny creature in a vast ocean, with only two other equally frightened people to keep him company. It occurred to him that Mr Rigger might have thought they were already on board and that any moment Ben would see the sails pulled out and the ship gather speed. And if that happened, how long would it be before they were missed? There was a muster call later in the afternoon; they would certainly be missed then, but that was some hours off and it would take the ship a long time to retrace its course to find them. By then it could be too late, as they would not be able to keep afloat indefinitely.

Ben thought this, and in fact it was exactly what

"But they are there, nonetheless, lurking way down below where the light never penetrates and it's dark and gloomy."

The Captain authorised swimming parties, with each deck being allowed to take it in turns to have a dip from the side of the ship.

"Try not to panic," Badger called out. "Save your strength to keep afloat."

the other two boys were thinking. None of them said anything about it, though – each was alone with his nightmare.

"Let's start swimming towards the ship," said Thomas. "Don't thrash around in the water – swim slowly and firmly. I'm sure they'll turn back soon."

Ben and Badger did as he suggested, and as they swam Badger told them what had happened to him once in Maine.

"I went swimming at the beach one day," he said. "Usually that beach is safe enough, but that day there was a rip. Do you know what a rip is?"

Thomas did, but Ben did not, so Badger explained. "It's a strong current that flows back out to sea," he said. "It carries you along with it and it's really strong. You can't swim back to the beach once you're in a rip – you'll just exhaust yourself and drown."

"So what do you do?" asked Ben, trying hard not to feel any current in the water around them.

"You let it carry you along," said Badger. "Then you swim out of it once it slackens. That's what happened to me. I survived."

"Obviously," said Thomas Seagrape. "Otherwise you wouldn't be able to tell this story, would you?"

As they were having this conversation, up on the deck of the *Tobermory*, Mr Rigger's attention had been attracted by Henry, who was standing at the stern, looking out at the sea and barking as loudly as he could. Everybody was used to Henry doing this from time to time – particularly when he thought he saw a mermaid – and for the most part they ignored it. But this time there was something in the tone of the dog's bark that made Mr Rigger uneasy.

"Have you seen something, Henry?" he asked, going over to stand beside him. As he asked this question, he looked down at the water behind their wake, and what he saw made him gasp in horror.

"Swing her round," he called to the person at the helm. "Hard to port!" Shouting out orders that the sails should be dropped, he immediately started the ship's engines and rushed to take control of the wheel. This took some time, but it soon became apparent to the boys in the water that they had been seen and that help was on its way.

"We're safe!" exclaimed Thomas. "They're coming back for us."

Had they not been in the water, Ben would have jumped for joy; as it was, all that he could manage to do was to stop swimming for a moment and clap his hands together as energetically as he could. Badger did the same thing, as did Thomas.

Captain Macbeth had now come up on deck and stood beside Mr Rigger at the helm.

"Carry on, Mr Rigger," he said. "I'm here if you need me."

With all the skill of an experienced helmsman, Mr Rigger guided the ship towards the three boys. Then, stopping the engine so that they would be in no danger from the propeller, he ordered a boat to be lowered. This was rowed across to where they were doggy-paddling in the water. Matron, who was in charge of the boat, reached down and hauled each one up in turn, spluttering like half-drowned rats. Then, with all three safe, the crew rowed them safely back to the *Tobermory*.

At dinner that night, all eyes were on the three boys.

"You were really lucky," said Poppy. "That could have turned out very differently."

"Well, it didn't," pronounced Ben. "And that's the important thing. Thanks to Henry."

"A giant squid could have eaten you," Tanya chipped in.

"Well, it didn't," said Badger, echoing Ben. "So what's the point of worrying about something that didn't happen?"

Nobody could think of an answer to that, so nothing more was said about it. That night, though, Ben dreamt that he was in the sea all by himself, miles and miles from land, with not a ship in sight. It was not a pleasant dream, and when he woke he was pleased to find himself in his hammock, being gently rocked by the movement of the ship. It was a safe, secure feeling, and he felt even safer when he looked across the cabin in the dark and saw Badger in his hammock, which was also swinging ever so slightly as the *Tobermory* made its way across the empty ocean, blown on its course by the warm wind from Africa.

CHAPTER 7

Ready-made knots

With the wind in their sails they made good progress across the wide Atlantic. Some of the young people on the *Tobermory* had done an ocean crossing before, but for Ben and Fee it was all new, and even those days when nothing much happened seemed exciting enough to them.

"I could do this forever," Ben said to his sister, when they were talking together on deck one morning. "Isn't it wonderful, Fee? Being out here, so far from everything, with just the sea all about us?"

Fee agreed. She loved the open sea and she loved being there with her friends. "I don't want this voyage to end," she said. "It's just perfect."

Of course it was not all just fun. The *Tobermory* was, after all, a school as well as a ship, and they had normal classes to attend. Each morning after breakfast, once they had finished the tasks assigned to them – scrubbing the decks, trimming the sails, and so on – they all filed into the ship's classrooms for the day's lessons. Because there were too many people to fit into a single room, they were divided into groups, each named after the points of the compass. So there was North Group, which included Fee, Poppy and Angela, and which would do maths, whilst South Group, in which Badger, Ben and Thomas found themselves, would do science. In the meantime, East Group would be studying oceanography with Miss Worsfold while West Group would be hard at work in Mr O'Brian's history class.

While classes were in progress, there were always some people who were excused because they were on duty, serving what was called a watch. These people would spend the whole morning on deck, attending to the ropes and sails or helping the helmsman and navigator to keep the ship going in the right direction. They did that for three days, and then it was somebody else's turn and they went back to the classroom. Most people enjoyed every minute of their watch. Sometimes something exciting would happen – there would be a sudden squall or gust of wind, perhaps, or they would see another ship – but for the most part it was a simple routine which many of them, including Ben and Fee, felt they were beginning to master.

Then there was lunch, which marked the end of classes, or at least of classes in the ordinary school subjects – *land subjects*, as they called them. In the afternoon there would be more instruction, but this was always connected with the business of sailing. These classes, known as *sea training*, were always held in small groups of five or six people, and were always very practical.

"We're not telling you how to do things," said Mr Rigger. "We're *showing* you how to do them."

One of the most popular subjects was knots, which was taught by Mr Rigger himself. It was said that as a young man he had been the champion knot-tier of the Royal Navy, but nobody knew whether this was true or not. Mr Rigger was too modest to confirm or deny it, and simply smiled when asked directly. "Can't say yes, can't say no," he would reply. But if you watched him tying a knot, you were left in no doubt at all that here was a real expert.

"Show us how fast you can tie a bowline, sir," Badger asked one afternoon. "They say that you're …"

Even before Badger could finish his sentence, there was a flurry of rope and hands and there before them, beautifully tied, was the famous bowline knot – a circle that looked rather like the end of a cowboy's lasso.

Badger whistled in admiration. "That was fast, sir!" he exclaimed.

"If you practise, you'll be just as fast," said Mr

Rigger, with a smile. "Now, everybody pay attention and I'll show you how to do it."

He took a length of rope and made a circle with one end. "Now," he said, "this goes in here, over there, through that, and then down again ... like so!"

Badger, Ben and Thomas painstakingly followed what Mr Rigger had done, holding their breath to see if they had done it correctly. They had, but it had taken them a long time and they knew that when you needed to tie a bowline at sea you might not have much time to do it. Yet with practice it would come to them, and they hoped that by the end of the voyage Mr Rigger would be proud of how quickly they could tie their knots.

Everybody enjoyed working with knots and they all looked forward to the knot competition that would be held a few days before they made landfall in Antigua, the island that was to be their first port of call in the Caribbean. This competition was held every time the *Tobermory* crossed an ocean, and it was always hotly contested. There were two prizes: one went to the person who tied a series of knots correctly and more quickly than anybody else, and the other went to the deck that did best overall. On the last long voyage the winners had been Upper Deck, which meant that the person who had stepped forward to receive the prize was none other than William Edward Hardtack, as Head Prefect of that deck.

"It was awful," Badger told Ben. "We all had to stand there and see Hardtack holding up the trophy and smirking. He was so pleased with himself."

"Just watching it," said Poppy, "was enough to make me feel sick."

"Do you think Upper Deck are going to win again?" asked Ben.

Poppy shrugged. "Who knows? I'm going to do my best to make sure that Middle Deck wins, but you can never be sure."

Ben was thoughtful. He had been working hard at his knots, but he was not sure how proficient he could become in the time. He would do his best, but he was worried about letting the whole deck down if he got things wrong. And it was so easy, he felt, to get things wrong when there were so many twists and turns in even the simplest knot.

Badger sensed his friend's concern. "Don't worry," he said. "A competition is only a competition – and it doesn't really matter if Upper Deck wins."

"No," said Ben, trying to convince himself. "It doesn't."

They looked at one another, and Ben laughed. "Although …" he began.

Badger finished the sentence for him. "Although I really hope they don't."

On the morning of the competition Ben and Badger

were up early. Out on deck they had only the few bleary-eyed members of the night's last watch for company. These were the people who had been on duty in the hours before dawn, sailing the ship through the darkness. They would soon be replaced by a fresh watch, although that would not happen until after breakfast.

The two boys sat at the edge of the deck, their feet over the side. If they leaned forward they could see the water slipping past. But they were not there to look at the sea, they were there to practise their knots. As the sun rose over the horizon like a huge red ball lifting itself out of the water, they tied and re-tied their practice rope, rehearsing the steps needed to make the perfect bowline, the most reliable cleat hitch, the most effective sheet bend. These are the knots that sailors need every day, and learning them was an important part of a *Tobermory* education.

Ben and Badger tested each other, making sure that every knot was faultless. Then, using Ben's wrist-watch, they timed themselves. Ben could tie a bowline in eight seconds; Badger could do a cleat hitch in three. And a round turn and two half hitches – a very useful knot for tying boats to mooring posts – took neither of them much more than twenty seconds. They were just as quick with other knots too.

"I think we've practised enough," said Badger eventually. "I could tie these knots in my sleep, I think!"

Ben agreed. He had just finished tying a bowline with his eyes shut – an important exercise, as there are times when you might have to tie a knot in the dark. But there comes a point when to practise more just makes you begin to doubt what you've learned, and so he too thought it time to stop.

They went down below to wash. Then, once everybody had finished their breakfast, Mr Rigger summoned them on deck for the competition.

"Pay attention, everybody," he began. "In a minute we will issue you all with fifteen pieces of string. Take good care of these, because if you lose any they will not be replaced. Then you will each receive a piece of paper on which you will find the names of fifteen knots. You are to tie these knots, using the string with which you've been issued. Is that clear?"

There was a general nodding of heads.

"The moment you finish your knots," said Mr Rigger, "report immediately to Matron or Miss Worsfold, who will be standing here beside me. Show them your knots and they will enter the time on their record sheet. In that way we'll know who takes how long to do the test." He looked out over the sea of heads. "Is that clear too?"

Again everybody nodded.

"So," said Mr Rigger, "find a place to sit and you will be given your string and the exam sheet. But don't start to tie anything until I blow my whistle."

Ben, Badger and Thomas all sat together on the foredeck, while Poppy, Fee, Tanya and Angela found a place near the main mast. They all received their string and their test sheet, and waited nervously for Mr Rigger's whistle. That came at last, and everybody began to tie knots as fast as they possibly could. Most people started with the easy knots – the cleat hitch and the sheet bend – but some tackled the more complicated knots right at the beginning.

Ben had tied seven knots when he heard Geoffrey Shark shout. "Finished!" came the triumphant cry, as the boy leapt to his feet and ran across the deck to Matron. And then, only a few seconds later, William Edward Hardtack did exactly the same thing, followed a few moments later by Maximilian Flubber.

Badger glanced at Ben. "How can they be finished?" he hissed. "I've only done eight."

Ben was too busy to think carefully about a reply, and what came out was automatic. "They've cheated," he said. "They must have."

"I bet you're right," said Thomas Seagrape. "Nobody could tie knots so quickly – not even Mr Rigger."

Matron entered the name of each of the boys in her notebook, along with the time. Then she passed the knots to Mr Rigger for inspection. He looked doubtful at first but as he checked each knot he nodded his approval. "Correct," he muttered. "And this one too – correct. Correct. Correct."

As their handiwork was approved, Hardtack and his friends stood with their arms folded, smirking with self-satisfaction.

"It makes me feel sick to see this," said Thomas.

"Me too," agreed Badger. "Something's wrong here – something just doesn't add up."

When time was up, Mr Rigger clapped his hands and everybody handed in their knots, finished or not. Scores were then allocated, and Mr Rigger, assisted by Miss Worsfold and Matron, added them up.

There was silence as Mr Rigger announced the results. "The individual winners," he said, "are as follows: in first place, William Edward Hardtack."

There was complete silence for a moment. Then Geoffrey Shark and Maximilian Flubber cheered. This led to a few half-hearted cheers from the rest of the members of Upper Deck, although it was clear that their hearts were not in it.

"Second place," said Mr Rigger, "goes to Geoffrey Shark, also of Upper Deck. And third place to Maximilian Flubber. Well done, boys – it means that the overall winner is Upper Deck. A very creditable performance, I must say."

"*Incredible* performance," whispered Badger. "Unbelievable, in fact, in the sense of being beyond belief."

Ben smiled wryly. "Do you think people get

pleasure out of winning something when they've cheated? Do you think you can actually feel good if you've won something dishonestly?"

Badger thought about this. "I suppose it depends on what you're like inside," he said at last. "If you're rotten inside, then I think you might be quite pleased to have won – even if you've cheated."

The competition over, everybody began to disperse. And that was when Thomas made his discovery. He was standing at the edge of the deck when he suddenly bent down to examine something that had caught his attention. He thought for a few moments and then beckoned his friends over to join him.

"Found something?" asked Badger.

Thomas indicated that they should all huddle together so as to be able to talk without being noticed. "Look at this," he said, holding out his hand.

"It's string," said Badger. "Just like the string we used for the knot test."

"That's exactly what it is," said Thomas. "Look, let's count the pieces."

Carefully separating each piece of string, Thomas began the count, finishing with "... forty-three, forty-four ..." He reached the final piece. "Forty-five."

He looked at his friends and repeated the number. "Forty-five."

Ben frowned. Thomas evidently thought this number was significant, but he couldn't see why.

"Three fifteens are?" said Thomas.

"Forty-five," answered Badger.

"And how many knots did we have to tie?" asked Thomas.

"Fifteen," said Ben. And then it dawned on him. "Oh …" He drew in his breath. "Who was standing here during the test?"

Thomas nodded. "Hardtack and Co. They were right here, exactly where I found the string. They must have dropped them."

Badger let out a low whistle. "So that's how they did it," he said. "They must have tied all the knots in advance, brought them along with them, then just not used the pieces of string that were handed out for the test."

"The cheats!" hissed Thomas. "The great big, sneaky, dishonest, low-down cheats!"

Ben wondered what they could do.

"Tell Mr Rigger," suggested Badger.

Thomas thought that this was the right thing to do. "We'll show him the string," he said. "That's our proof."

They found Mr Rigger in the staffroom, drinking a cup of tea along with Matron and Miss Worsfold.

"So what do we have here?" enquired Mr Rigger. "A deputation?"

"We'd like to talk about the knot competition," said Thomas.

Mr Rigger smiled. "I hope you enjoyed it," he said.

Badger intervened. "Yes, we did, sir, but …" He trailed off.

Mr Rigger looked concerned. "But what?"

"But we don't think it was fair," said Ben.

Mr Rigger glanced at Matron and Miss Worsfold. "But we were all watching very carefully, weren't we, ladies? It didn't seem unfair to us."

Matron shook her head. "All above board, I'd say."

Mr Rigger turned back to face the boys. "You'll have to explain, I think."

Thomas stepped forward. He held out the bundle of string. "We found this," he said.

Mr Rigger looked at the string with a puzzled expression. "This is string," he said.

"We found it where Hardtack and his friends had been standing," he said.

This did not help Mr Rigger. "Well?" he said.

"I think they cheated, sir," chipped in Badger.

Mr Rigger looked at Badger severely. "That's a very serious allegation," he said. "Tell me why you think that."

Badger explained their theory. When he had finished, Mr Rigger looked thoughtful and stroked his moustache, which was always a sign that he was thinking very hard. At length he spoke. "Possible," he said. "It's just possible, but …" He hesitated. "But I'm afraid that we just don't have any proof."

"We have the string," blurted out Thomas.

Mr Rigger shook his head. "That's not enough," he said. "That could have been dropped by anybody."

The boys looked at one another. It was always the same when it came to the misdeeds of Hardtack and his gang. Proof – there was never enough proof, and as a result he and his friends got away with everything.

It was Matron who spoke next. "I think Mr Rigger is right," she said. "But I must say it gives me no pleasure to say so."

"And I feel the same," said Miss Worsfold. "Sorry, boys."

Ben, Badger and Thomas all felt disappointed as they walked back to the companionway that led to their deck. As they did so, they heard a voice calling them. "Hey, you!"

They turned round. William Edward Hardtack had appeared from round a corner, and behind him were standing Geoffrey Shark and Maximilian Flubber.

"Yes?" asked Thomas.

"What were you doing in the staffroom?" challenged Hartack. "Telling tales?"

"Mind your own business," retorted Badger.

Hardtack took a step forward. "But it is my business, Stripey. It's very much my business if people like you go in there ..." He gestured towards the staffroom door before continuing, "... to tell lies about other people."

Badger laughed. "Lies? You're the one who should know all about that, Hardtack."

"You hear that?" said Geoffrey Shark. "You hear that, Tacky? That creep is calling you a liar."

"I heard it," said Hardtack. "I heard it, Geoff."

He was about to say something more but he was interrupted. The staffroom door had opened and Mr Rigger came out, followed by Matron and Miss Worsfold. There was an immediate change in Hardtack's manner.

"Oh, good evening, Mr Rigger," he said, his voice dripping with insincerity. "And good evening, Matron and Miss Worsfold."

The teachers looked at him and acknowledged his greeting, although none of them seemed too pleased to see him.

"Let's go," said Badger. "No point in staying around here."

And with that they walked off. They all felt a strong sense of disappointment. Witnessing an act of dishonesty can be unpleasant; you feel somehow disappointed, somehow saddened. And you may hope – hope very much – that somebody will come and put things right. But sometimes nobody comes.

In Green Island Bay

It was Ben who heard the voices first. He was still asleep in his hammock, but had just entered that strange state between deep sleep and wakefulness – that time when your eyes are still closed but you are vaguely aware of what is happening around you. You may still be dreaming, though, and Ben was. He was back in Tobermory, he thought, standing on the harbour wall, and there was a talking seagull – which proved that it really was a dream. The seagull was trying to tell him something, but Ben was having trouble making out exactly what it was. And then a dog came – a strange, spotted dog – and chased the seagull away.

As the voices grew louder, the dream faded, and when he opened his eyes he saw that he was in his cabin, not on the harbour wall at Tobermory, and that there, opposite him, was Badger in his hammock, one arm hanging lazily down as if he was about to pick something up off the cabin floor.

"Badge?" said Ben. "Badge, did you hear something?"

From Badger's side of the cabin there came a strange noise. It could have been a word, or it could just have been the sort of grunt that says *I'm still asleep*. But then the sound of voices drifted down again from the deck above, and both boys half-sat up in their hammocks. (You can only half-sit up in a hammock, as if you try to sit up straight you wobble and can end up on the floor.)

"What was that?" asked Badger, rubbing the sleep from his eyes.

"It's morning," replied Ben, noticing the faint light coming through their porthole. "And that sounds like the night watch shouting."

"Perhaps it's just because their watch is over," said Badger.

But the pitch of the shouting grew higher, and the boys realised that something important must be happening up above. And then in a moment they heard what it was. "Land!" shouted a voice quite clearly now. "Land ahoy!"

Ben and Badger wasted no time. For the last few days the whole school had known they were drawing near to the Caribbean, and at last they had arrived. At some point in the night they must have crossed that invisible boundary where the North Atlantic Ocean became the Caribbean. And the land that somebody had spotted would be Antigua, the island that was their first destination. It was a great moment and the boys wanted to be on deck to share in it.

And so did everybody else. By the time Ben and Badger had thrown on their clothes and raced up the companionway, the deck was filled with people, some in their day uniforms, others still in their pyjamas and dressing gowns. Everybody was crowding at the railings, straining their eyes to see the distant smudge on the horizon that was Antigua.

Ben and Badger found themselves standing near Poppy and Fee.

"I thought we'd arrive this morning," said Poppy. "I was looking at the charts yesterday and I worked out how far we had to go."

Poppy was particularly good at navigation. She liked using the dividers on the charts to measure distances; she loved rotating the clear plastic compass that allowed her to measure angles; she took great pleasure in poring over all the printed symbols that meant rocks and shipwrecks and lighthouses.

"I can't wait," said Fee. "I can't wait to anchor in ..." She tried to remember exactly where they were going. If Poppy was particularly good at navigation and at remembering places, Fee was the opposite.

"In Green Island Bay," said Ben. "That's where the Captain said we were going."

"I've seen a photograph of it," said Poppy. "It's a great place to anchor. You can swim with turtles and go kitesurfing, if you like. And there's a small harbour nearby with some houses and a shop."

The wind was strong. It was a warm wind, though – not the sort of wind that makes you want to be inside. It was the kind of wind that caresses your face with its salty fingers and then blows through your hair in a friendly way. It was a wind that could carry a sailing ship smoothly and quickly over the waves, and that is exactly what it did now. With every minute that passed, the tiny blob on the horizon got bigger. Soon they could make out cliffs, and hills behind them. Then the hills became better defined, and they could see trees and buildings, presumably houses, but which were still just tiny white dots at this distance.

Captain Macbeth was now at the helm. The last watch – those people who had spent the last four hours of the night on duty – had now been told to go below, eat the early breakfast Cook had prepared for them, and try to get some sleep. They knew that would be difficult, though, as nobody wanted to miss the excitement of making landfall, but an order from the Captain was an order that nobody could disobey, and they all made their way reluctantly below.

The Captain called Thomas Seagrape over to his side. "Well, Thomas," he said. "I know this isn't

Jamaica, but it's still the Caribbean. So it must feel a little bit like coming home."

Thomas nodded. "It does, Captain. I've been here before, you know – quite a few times – on my mum's boat."

The Captain nodded. "I thought you might have. And so I wondered whether you would like to be at the wheel when we come in, with me standing right behind you, just in case."

It was the biggest compliment that the captain of a ship can pay – to offer the helm to somebody – and Thomas could not conceal his delight. Stepping forward, he squared his shoulders and took his place behind the great wheel that guided the ship.

"Keep her on this course," said the Captain. "That'll take us nice and straight into Green Island Bay."

Ben and Badger watched in admiration as Thomas steered the great ship. They could not stay for long, though, as breakfast was about to be served, but Thomas, and anybody else on duty on deck, would have hot bread rolls, filled with bacon or jam, brought up to them, together with a mug of steaming hot chocolate.

Distances over water can be deceptive. Something which looks close can actually be much further away than you think. So even after land had been sighted, the *Tobermory* still had a good few nautical miles to cover before it reached Green Island Bay. But eventually they arrived, and the order was given to drop the sails. Because the entrance to the bay was narrow, it would be safer to go in under engine power, so standing behind Thomas, the Captain gave orders for that to be done. Speaking to the engine room through a long rubber tube, he told them: "Start engines: half-speed ahead."

Once again the whole school was on deck, excitedly pointing out features on the land.

"Look at that house!" exclaimed Tanya, pointing to a building perched on the very edge of a cliff. "If Matron lived there she'd be able to dive straight out of her window into the sea."

"And look at that one," she said as they sailed past a house on the edge of a small beach. "The sea probably comes into your bedroom at high tide."

"I'd love to live here," said Fee. "I'd love to be able to walk out of my house and dive straight into the sea whenever I wanted to. And look at the colour of the water – look at that amazing green."

She was right. The green, everybody agreed, was extraordinary – and when water is that colour you want to jump straight in. It was the colour of an emerald, only a bit lighter.

The water became shallower. Leaning over the railing, Angela Singh spotted sand down below and called out to the others in her excitement. They peered down and saw, far beneath them, the white sand, mottled here and there with dark patches of seaweed.

"That's a good thirty feet," said Tanya. "The water's so clear here you can see right down."

The ship slowed down now, as the shore was not far off and there were rocks. On one of the outcrops of rock, half covered by the breaking wavelets, was the wreck of an old ship – a warning, if one were needed, to sailors to be careful of the reefs and currents.

Ben was fascinated. He had never seen such exciting and appealing waters, and he could hardly wait for the chance to swim. Ben was imagining what it would be like to swim amongst the fish in the clear warm water when he suddenly noticed something. At first he thought it was a fishing float that somebody had dropped – a round, bobbing piece of cork – but then, when he looked again he saw that it was something quite different.

"A turtle!" he cried. "Look – a turtle!"

Badger was soon at his side, peering in the direction in which Ben was pointing. "There it is!" he shouted. "And it's a big one."

The turtle was swimming directly towards the *Tobermory* but suddenly it stopped, looked up, and dived. For a few moments it could still be seen, a light brown blob under the water, and then it was gone. And now another creature had arrived to inspect the new arrivals – a large brown bird with an elegant long neck and beak.

"That's a booby," said Poppy. "I've seen one before. A lot of people think they bring good luck."

They watched as the bird circled the *Tobermory*. They felt its eyes on them and all of them, in their different ways, wondered what good luck the booby might bring. Badger thought of his parents: good luck for him would mean they might find a bit more time for him. Tanya thought of her father, and of a possible reunion with him. Ben thought of Hardtack and his gang: good luck might bring justice and the exposure of the sheer nastiness of that unfriendly trio. For a moment he allowed himself to think of Hardtack being made to walk the plank, as they would do in the old pirate days. Walking the plank was a terrible fate, as sharks would be waiting below. Ben would never wish that on anybody, but if Hardtack were made to walk the plank and given a good soaking before being picked up and brought back on board, then it might make him think about mending his ways.

The excitement they all felt was now mounting. But they didn't have time to sit and talk; anchoring *Tobermory* involved not only the dropping of the ship's great anchor, but also the stowing away of ropes, the fastening of sail covers, the preparation of shore boats, and a general tidying up of the decks.

Everybody had something to do, and in no time at all – or so it seemed – they were at anchor, not far off a beach, with the great sweep of Green Island Bay behind them. It was an ideal spot to spend a few days. It had been hard work getting across the vast ocean, and now, they hoped, there would be a little time simply to have some fun.

And there would be fun. Shortly after, Captain Macbeth called the whole ship's company to a muster on deck. Standing with Mr Rigger on one side of him and Matron on the other, he told them what lay ahead.

"Now listen," he began, which was the way he often started his talks. "This is the plan." That was another thing he said rather a lot. "We are going to spend a whole week here. Then we are going to sail south, to an island called Dominica. We shall spend three weeks there while normal lessons take place. But before that, I want you all to enjoy yourselves as much as possible."

This brought a cheer, with several caps being thrown in the air.

"So we've laid on various activities," the Captain continued. "Matron here is going to be running diving lessons – if you're interested, sign up with her."

Matron gave a nod. "Anybody can learn to dive," she said. "Whatever shape you are, there's a dive for everybody."

"And then," the Captain said, "there's kitesurfing. As you may know, kitesurfing is a really exciting sport and …" He hesitated, and then pointed over the starboard side of the ship. "And here's a kitesurfer coming towards us right now."

Every eye looked to the right to see a large kite filled with the breeze coming towards them at what seemed like an alarming speed. The kite was tethered by lines, and these lines led down to a trapeze grasped by a woman on a small surfboard. This surfboard was cutting through the water like a powerboat, leaving a wake in the water behind it. As the kitesurfer approached, she suddenly pulled on the kite strings and changed direction, heading back out towards the open sea.

"You see," said the Captain. "How's that for fun? And lessons, I'm happy to say, will be given to all those who want to learn. The instructor will be Miss Worsfold. Miss Worsfold," he added, "is a very good kitesurfer. She took part in the World Kitesurfing Championships some years ago in Mexico and came eleventh overall."

That last bit of information had been a surprise. The teachers on the *Tobermory* were all very capable, but nobody knew just how good they were at various things. There was a loud cheer. Miss Worsfold was popular, and there would be a long list of people eager to try kitesurfing.

"In addition," the Captain went on, "there will be snorkelling, long-distance swimming, and kayaking." He paused. "Safety first, of course. Always look before you jump into the water. Check there are no rocks down below. Don't pester any turtles or fish – they have their own lives to lead and they don't want you interfering."

Matron made her contribution too. "Wear plenty of sunscreen," she said. "It's available from the sick bay. And don't touch coral – it can be sharp, and a coral graze takes a long time to heal. Also, wash the salt out of your hair after swimming. Is that clear?"

Everyone nodded their heads, and with that the Captain dismissed them.

"Kitesurfing for me," said Badger. "I've seen it done up in Maine, but I've never had the chance to do it myself."

"And for me," said Ben.

In addition to diving, Poppy was keen to do some snorkelling, and would be joined in that by Angela and Tanya, even if they were still a bit nervous of the water. Fee was keen to have diving lessons with Matron – she had already mastered the basics and wanted to try more demanding dives. Everybody, it seemed, had something they really wanted to do. There were still a few hours of daylight left, so there was no reason why activities should not start straight-away. Miss Worsfold led a large group off for their first kitesurfing class, while Matron climbed high up into the rigging and started to perform display dives for her class down below.

The kitesurfing class was not only interesting, but challenging too. The highlight, though, of the introductory session – at least for Badger and Ben – was when Geoffrey Shark, who had pushed himself forward to be the first to have a go, was caught in a sudden gust of wind and whisked up into the air, surfboard and all, and carried along for a good distance.

The wind dropped suddenly and he fell like a stone into the water. Shark was unhurt, but his dignity had taken a tumble, and he looked embarrassed and surly when he swam back to the beach.

"You weren't listening to me, Geoffrey," scolded Miss Worsfold. "You did it all wrong, and that's why you were picked up in the air like that."

Shark stared down at the sand, ashamed and angry. And he was angrier still when Badger, who was next up, managed a perfect circle round the bay at great speed, the kite completely under his control. He was roundly congratulated by Miss Worsfold on his return.

"That's exactly how it should be done," she said. Turning to Shark, she said, rather sharply, "And Geoffrey, I hope you were watching how Badger did it. If you can do it half as well as that, you'll be making great progress."

"Land!" shouted a voice quite clearly now. "Land ahoy!"

"That's a booby," said Poppy. "I've seen one before. A lot of people think they bring good luck."

"Shark was caught in a sudden gust of wind and whisked up into the air, surfboard and all ..."

William Edward Hardtack was not in the class to support him, so Shark just glowered and said nothing. But Badger knew that this would be reported back later on, and that it would probably be made worse in the telling. That worried him; Hardtack was capable of anything, and Badger had no wish to provoke him unnecessarily. *Don't poke a rattlesnake with a stick*, he thought.

Of course all of the day's activities were tiring, and that night everybody felt far too exhausted to talk very much after lights-out.

Ben and Badger had a conversation though, although it came to a sudden end when Badger dropped off to sleep mid-sentence.

"I like it here," said Ben drowsily.

"Me too," murmured Badger.

"I never want this to end," Ben continued.

"Me too," said Badger, barely audible now. "I really like …"

And that was it. Sleep claimed him, and Ben was not to hear what his friend really liked. But he could imagine what it was. It was everything.

Meeting Mike

After breakfast the following morning, when Poppy and Fee were busy scrubbing the deck, the two girls noticed a small, brightly painted boat making its way towards them across the bay. They had already seen a few such boats that morning – they were used by local people for fishing, or getting from one side of the bay to the other, or, in some cases, for going up to visiting ships to sell them fish, fruit and vegetables.

At first they thought that this was one of those boats, but as it drew closer they recognised that it was different. This boat had no wares on board to sell and seemed to be quite empty, apart from the person at the tiller. As the boat drew closer, they realised that the figure at the tiller was a boy, who was waving as he approached.

Mr Rigger was in charge on the deck. He had spotted the approaching boat too, and gave Poppy and Fee the order to lower the ladder so the boy could come aboard.

Mike Wood

"Ahoy there!" Poppy shouted as they dropped the ladder that enabled visitors to come aboard the *Tobermory*. "Who are you and what do you want?"

"Ahoy there, *Tobermory*!" came the reply. "I'm Mike Wood and I have a message for the Captain."

"Tie up and come aboard," shouted Poppy. This was the correct thing to say, as the sea is an hospitable place, and you should always invite a visitor aboard unless you have a very good reason not to do so.

The two girls watched as Mike tied up his boat and began to make his way up the ladder. They saw that he was a boy of about their own age, and judging by the speed with which he secured his boat and climbed up the rungs, they could tell that he must spend a lot of time on the water. As he came up on deck they noticed a few more things about him: his smile, which was broad and friendly, his clothes, which had obviously seen a lot of hard work, and the fact that he was not wearing any shoes.

Mike held out his hand. "Well," he said, "you know my name, but I don't know yours."

They introduced themselves, and he shook their hands warmly.

"Do you live here?" asked Poppy.

Mike gestured over his shoulder. "Yes, I live back there. You see that place over there on the shore? That's our house."

Poppy and Fee looked over his shoulder to where he was pointing. It was a very small house – not much more than a shack really – but it was right on the beach, with swaying palm trees behind it.

"I live there with my mother and my younger sister," Mike went on. "We catch fish. Well, I do most of the fishing these days; my mother sells it to the hotel and to boats that come by here."

As he spoke, the girls noticed that he was looking about him admiringly.

"This is our school ship," said Poppy. "We sail around while we go to school. Otherwise, it's the same as any school really. Same as yours, I imagine."

Mike shook his head. It seemed to Poppy that her question had saddened him. "I don't go to school," he said. "I used to, but not anymore."

Poppy and Fee were unsure what to say. They were trying to imagine what it would be like not to have a school to go to. Some people might think that rather nice, but it was clear that Mike did not.

"You've got a message for the Captain?" Poppy asked.

"Yes," said Mike. "It's a letter from Captain Tommy, who knew your Captain years ago. I have to give it to him personally."

"Follow us," said Fee.

They took Mike down below and led him along the passageway to the Captain's cabin. Poppy knocked loudly and waited for the familiar voice to call them in.

"This boy has a message for you, Captain," said Poppy. "His name is Mike and the message is from …"

The Captain looked up from the logbook laid out on his desk. "I'm sure he can speak for himself, Poppy," he interrupted. Turning to Mike, he said, "Well, young man?"

Mike seemed nervous, fumbling as he took the envelope out of his pocket. Seeing this, Captain Macbeth tried to put him at his ease. "I've got a good idea who this letter might be from," he said, smiling. "My old friend, Captain Tommy?"

Mike relaxed. "Yes, sir," he said. "It's from Captain Tommy all right. He gave me the letter when he saw your ship sail in."

The Captain laughed. "I knew he'd be watching," he said. "Does he still sit in that chair of his and watch everything that happens in the bay?"

"Yes, sir," replied Mike. "I help him a bit these days. I go to the market for him and I painted his boat last year – not that he can go out to sea any more, now that he's … well, I don't know how old he is."

"I don't imagine he knows either," said the Captain as he slit open the envelope with his paper-knife.

He read the letter and then nodded. "Tell him that I'll come and see him tomorrow morning at six bells on the forenoon watch, just as he suggests."

Mike nodded. "He said that you could bring some of your crew, if you like."

"Did he now?" said the Captain. "Well, it would be nice for them to meet him, I think." He looked at Poppy and Fee. "You two, would you like to come?"

Poppy and Fee nodded enthusiastically.

"And bring a couple of the boys along as well," said the Captain.

"Ben and Badger," said Fee quickly. "Can they come too?"

"I don't see why not," said the Captain. "And Thomas Seagrape. I expect his mother will have come across Captain Tommy at some point. Tell Thomas to come along as well."

They left the Captain's cabin and walked with Mike back to the deck ladder. Their visitor seemed interested in everything, asking about where they had their meals, where they kept their hammocks, and what the teachers were like. Their answers seemed only to further rouse his curiosity, and he asked more and more questions. Then, just as he was about to climb down the ladder, he said, "You're really lucky, you know."

"Lucky?" asked Fee.

Mike thought for a moment before replying. "Yes, having this beautiful ship. Sailing off together and learning all sorts of things. That's really lucky, you know."

Poppy and Fee said nothing. He was right, they thought; it was just that there was nothing they could really say. Mike's life, they suspected, was not quite so lucky.

"I think I'll see you tomorrow at Captain Tommy's place," said Mike as he began his descent of the ladder. "And your friends too."

"We look forward to that," said Fee, waving. "Goodbye, Mike."

They watched as he climbed into his boat, started the outboard engine, and began his journey back across the bay. After a minute or so, he turned and waved to them, and they waved back.

"Did you feel a bit sad just then?" asked Fee as they returned to their work on the deck.

Poppy looked thoughtful. "Yes, I did." She paused. "But why? Why do you think we both felt sad?"

"Because ..." began Fee, and then stopped. "I'm not sure."

But Poppy had an idea. "I think it's because we

have something he doesn't," she said. "And that can make you feel sad. It just does."

"Even if not everybody can have the same things?" asked Fee.

"Yes," said Poppy. "I think Mike would love to go to school. I think he'd love to have the chance to study the things we study."

"Even though we also have to scrub the decks?" asked Fee.

Poppy smiled. "Even though we have to do that."

Fee sighed. "I suspect he'd be far better at it than we are."

Poppy agreed. "And catching fish too. He'll do lots of things rather well, I think."

"I wish he could join the school," said Fee. "Don't you think that would be great?"

"It would be," said Poppy. "But it's not going to happen, I'm afraid. Somebody has to pay for us to be on the *Tobermory* and I don't think Mike's family will have the money."

"I'm sorry about that," said Fee. "I wish we could help."

"Yes," said Poppy. She would have liked to have added something to that, but she could not think what to say. It is one thing to want to help; it is quite another to be able to do so.

Captain Macbeth had a special rowing boat reserved for his personal use. It was a fine boat, its hull painted dark blue with the rest of the woodwork dazzling white. The oars were of polished pine and cut into the water with hardly a splash – at least when used by good rowers. That morning Poppy and Fee were on the starboard oars and Ben and Badger on the port; Thomas Seagrape, wearing his smartest blue-and-white sailor outfit, was at the tiller, steering the boat expertly towards the shore. *No captain could wish for a better crew*, thought Captain Macbeth as he sat in the bows and watched his students at work.

As they approached the beach, they saw that Mike was already there to greet them. Wading out in his bare feet, he helped to bring the rowing boat up onto the sand where it would be safe from the tide. He had not met any of the boys yet, so he shook hands with each of them. Ben, who always felt that he could judge in a minute or two whether he was going to get on with somebody, was sure that Mike would become a firm friend.

"Captain Tommy told me to bring you straight up to the house," said Mike. "He's waiting for you."

They followed him along a path that led up from the beach towards the side of a hill. On this hillside, dotted around under the trees, were houses with bright red roofs. And the walls, too, were colourful – mostly greens and blues that matched the brilliant sky and sea. After a while the path led on to a narrow tarred road that climbed further up the hill in one direction and down to the harbour in the other.

"Not far now," said Mike, pointing to a single-storey house with light green walls set back from the road. "That's Captain Tommy's place."

They could tell that it was a sailor's house.

On the fence beside the gate was a fishing-net hung out across the posts, along with a collection of old fishing floats. Then, on the path that led to the front veranda, was an old wooden rowing boat, upturned so that its hull faced the sky, its name painted in a fancy script: *Nancy Blue*.

The veranda was partly hidden by a large flowering tree, and once they walked around that they saw Captain Tommy waiting for them. He was sitting on an ancient wickerwork chair, holding a walking stick in one hand and beckoning them enthusiastically with the other.

"Ahoy there, Captain Macbeth!" he called. "Ahoy there, *Tobermory* crew!"

Captain Macbeth bounded up the steps to greet his old friend. They shook hands firmly before Captain Tommy turned to greet each of the others in turn.

Poppy shook hands first. She was struck by Captain Tommy's piercing green eyes. She had never seen eyes like that before – other than in a Burmese

cat. Fee followed her. She noticed the old naval cap he wore and its intricate gold badge. She imagined how many high seas and storms that cap had seen.

Then it was the turn of the boys. They admired everything about Captain Tommy – the voice that sounded as deep as the sea itself; the wrinkled skin that looked as if it was made out of waterproof tarpaulin; and of course the proud, erect bearing that came from years of commanding sailors at sea. This was a man, they thought, who knew everything there was to know about the sea.

The two captains wanted some time alone to talk about old times, so Mike, at Captain Tommy's suggestion, took everybody else off to the kitchen at the back of the house for a glass of lemonade.

"Captain Tommy makes this himself from the lemons that grow in his garden," he said. "It's said to be the best lemonade in the entire Caribbean."

When they tasted it, everyone had to agree. Then Mike gave them each one of Captain Tommy's famous ship's biscuits. He explained these were made with coconut from the Captain's own trees. "They've won prizes up in Jamaica and down in Grenada," Mike said. "There are lots of people who would love to get their hands on the recipe."

They went outside to sit on the back veranda. There they talked for almost half an hour before Mike suggested they go back to see the two captains.

Captain Tommy and Captain Macbeth had finished talking about the old days and were pleased to see the crew.

"There's something I want to tell you people," said Captain Tommy. "I've already told young Wood here." He nodded towards Mike. "He knows the story – but I'd like you to know too."

"We'd love to hear it," said Poppy, speaking for all of them.

Captain Tommy nodded in her direction. "Well said, young lady. There are people who don't want to hear stories, but you'll never make true sailors out of them. Real sailors are always interested in a good story, as long as the sea comes into it somewhere. And it does in this one – in fact the sea is right at the heart of it.

"This all took place some time ago," he continued. "Your captain here, Captain Macbeth, was a very young man then – he was in command of his first ship, the *Puffin*. It was not a very big ship, but you never forget your first command, no matter how small she is.

"I was the captain of a steamer that sailed all the way down the Eastern Caribbean, stopping at a lot of the smaller islands. We delivered just about everything back then – trucks, spare parts, food, picks and shovels – you name it, we carried it.

"Now, there was a right nasty piece of work

hanging about in these waters – a man by the name of Thorn. Robert Algernon Thorn, to give him his full name, but he was generally known as Bert Thorn, or simply Thorn. Thorn was a crook. He used to have a racket in out-of-date pies in Jamaica, but they chased him out of Kingston after the pies made everyone ill, and he took to being a pirate.

"People think that pirates don't exist any longer. They think of Captain Morgan and the likes, and all that swashbuckling stuff from hundreds of years ago. But they forget that there are plenty of modern-day pirates who have all the latest equipment and chase after innocent boats to rob them of anything they can lay their hands on. Oh yes, there are still pirates all right, and Thorn was one of the worst.

"I had been lucky – I had never run into him, until one day I was about to put into harbour at a place called Pigeon Island. I suppose I wasn't paying enough attention, and I didn't spot Thorn's boat lurking by the headland. Well, he nipped out and before I knew where I was he had come alongside me and his men had boarded. They were armed to the teeth with guns and knives. And so I had no choice but to start handing over anything of value to the grinning Mr Thorn. 'Nice to meet you, Captain Tommy,' he sneered. 'And nicer still to relieve you of some of your bits and pieces.'

"There was nothing I could do, and I was resigned

to my fate when I saw, out of the corner of my eye, a boat sailing full tilt towards us. I wondered whether it was one of Thorn's band, but then I saw somebody I recognised at the helm. It was your own captain, my friends – your own Captain Macbeth.

"And you know what he did? He rammed Thorn's boat midships. There was an awful bump and sound of breaking timbers. Thorn jumped up like a scalded cat and ran to the side to see what was happening. Well, what we saw was his ship listing to port and beginning to sink. He let out a tremendous wail – I can still hear it if I close my eyes – and jumped back onto his stricken ship. I think he wanted to sail it to land, but he didn't get that far. From where I stood on deck I could see him getting lower and lower in the water and then, a good three hundred yards off the beach, his ship sank altogether. Thorn and his bunch of thugs had to swim through the breakers to reach the shore. They made a most bedraggled spectacle."

Captain Tommy paused in his story. "So it was your captain who saved me, my friends. I probably even owe my life to him."

Captain Macbeth looked embarrassed. "Oh, I don't know, Tommy. Anybody would have done what I did …"

"And he's modest as well as brave," said Captain Tommy.

"Oh, I'm not so sure about that," protested Captain Macbeth.

Captain Tommy now rose to his feet – rather hesitantly and with the aid of his walking stick. "Well, whatever you say, Macbeth, I owe you a lot, and that's why I'm going to give you my sea-chest. It's not much, but it's full of all sorts of things that I'll never have the energy to sort out. Perhaps you can get these fine young people here to help you. There might be stuff that some maritime museum somewhere would be interested in."

He indicated to Thomas, Ben and Mike that they should follow him, and then he went inside. A few minutes later the boys emerged behind him, carrying a large and clearly rather heavy wooden chest.

"I want you to take this and do what you think is the right thing with it," said Captain Tommy to Captain Macbeth. "Mike will help your crew to carry it down to your boat."

Captain Macbeth tried to persuade his friend to hold on to his treasures, but to no avail. "My sea-chest is of no interest to me now," said Captain Tommy. "You take it and see what you can do with it."

Captain Macbeth thanked him. He knew there are times when you have to accept a present gracefully, and this was one of them.

In the boat on the way back to the *Tobermory*, nobody could take their eyes off the old sea-chest.

What did it contain? Treasure of some sort – it was heavy enough for that – or just the old bits and pieces from a long seafaring life?

"Can we open the chest when we get back to the boat?" asked Poppy.

Captain Macbeth thought for a while. "You're all going to be busy with your activities. Perhaps in a day or two." Then he added, "Who's going kitesurfing today?"

Badger said that he had put his name down for Miss Worsfold's next kitesurfing class.

"It's very windy," said the Captain, looking up at the wispy white clouds scudding across the sky. "So be extra careful."

"I will," said Badger. He thought for a moment, and then asked the question he had wanted to ask Captain Tommy, but had not. "What happened to Bert Thorn?"

"After he swam ashore?"

"Yes. Was he arrested?"

Captain Macbeth shook his head. "He and his crew scarpered," he said. "That was all a long time ago. Nobody's ever seen or heard from him since, as far as I know." He looked thoughtful. "He wouldn't have been much good as a pirate once he'd lost his ship. So he's probably up to some other form of mischief now – who knows?"

CHAPTER
10

A dangerous moment

Lightning never strikes in the same place twice – or so the old saying goes. But sometimes these old sayings are just not true. So it was that Badger, who had already had a close escape from drowning when the ship sailed off without him and his fellow swimmers, should have been a bit more careful when kitesurfing that afternoon.

This is what happened. It was during Miss Worsfold's second kitesurfing class, when there were ten people all being instructed in the tricky art of standing up on a surfboard and being pulled along by a powerful and often unruly kite. It looks so easy when you see an expert doing it, but just try it for yourself. That is when you find out just how hard it is to stay upright on water.

Badger, though, as he had already demonstrated, was naturally good at it. Perhaps it was his sense of balance; perhaps it was because he had strong leg muscles; perhaps it was because some people are quick learners when it comes to new sports. Whatever the reason, Badger could kitesurf like a champion.

Miss Worsfold was most impressed. "I obviously have nothing to teach you, Badger," she said. "You can just go ahead and do it by yourself while I show the others. "But don't go too far out," she warned. "Remember the sea can get rough out there and can make it hard to turn round."

Badger promised her that he would be careful. Then, under the admiring eyes of the rest of the class, who had still to learn how to stand up on the board without falling into the water, he set off. There were several shouts and whistles as the wind caught the kite and drew it out above him. Like a bird soaring in a current of air, the kite billowed and pulled, tugging Badger on his board. Through the waves he cut, leaping and dipping on the green sea like a dancer.

"Look at that!" marvelled Miss Worsfold. "That boy is competition standard already."

She tore herself away from the inspiring sight of Badger on his board to continue her lesson. So she did not see – nor did anybody else – Badger shooting across the water at considerable speed, heading for the mouth of the bay where a line of breakers marked the position of the reef. Here the open sea met the line of coral and became a tumbling chaos of waves and foam. There was a break, though, in the reef – a channel through which boats could pass without risk of being dashed on the rocks – and it was towards this gap that the wind was pulling Badger.

An observer on the shore might have been worried that Badger would misjudge his position and be dragged onto the reef, but Badger had no such fear. He felt in complete control of the kite above him and he knew he could, by small movements of his wrists, by the slightest tugs and twists, send the straining kite off in the direction of his choosing. So now he lined himself up with the channel through the reef; he would pass through that, he thought, and then make a wide turn in the open sea beyond. Afterwards he would come back through the channel and surf right up to the beach where Miss Worsfold was teaching the group. It would be a triumphant return.

But sometimes things do not go quite as planned. Although Badger made it safely through the gap in the reef, once he was out in the open sea he found himself in conditions that were altogether much rougher. Now, with much larger waves to contend with, all his effort was focused on staying on the board. He knew that one miscalculation, one momentary loss of concentration, would see him tumble headlong into the water. And he was not at all sure that he would be able to get back on the board in those conditions – in fact, he was sure he would not. That would leave him floundering in the large waves and carried back towards the reef and its razor-sharp rocks. Not even the strongest, most experienced swimmer would be able to avoid being cut to ribbons if that happened.

No, he thought, he would have to concentrate on getting as far away from the reef as possible. That meant staying on his current course, further out into the open sea. At least when he was out there if he should come off the board he would not be in such immediate danger, unless, of course … no, he could not bear to think about sharks right now. Sharks tend not to come inside a reef, so you are usually safe if you stay there. But the open sea is a different matter.

Badger might have been all right had the wind not suddenly increased. But as it rose, he found himself going faster and faster. Glancing over his shoulder, he saw the land receding behind him. The beach was now not much more than a thin line of yellow, with Miss Worsfold and her class a few indistinct dots. He was now surrounded by larger waves, rolling in off the Atlantic, some of them beginning to curl and break at the top. Riding these waves was a stomach-churning experience and controlling the kite above his head was beginning to take its toll on his shoulders and arms. He wanted more than anything to let go of the trapeze – to let the kite fly away – and to sink into the water. But if he did that he would be unable to swim against the current, invisible to anybody on land. It suddenly dawned on Badger that he might die. *This is happening to me*, he thought. *This is not something I'm watching in a movie; this is real.*

And then he saw it. Not far away, coming straight towards him, was a small, brightly painted boat, propelled through the waves by an outboard motor. And at the tiller was somebody who, even from this distance, he recognised. Mike!

In no time at all Mike was just behind him, following his course but leaving just enough room between them so that they would not collide.

"Let go!" shouted Mike over the whistling of the wind. "Let go of the kite and I'll pick you up."

For a moment Badger was confused. If he let go, the kite would simply fly away and he would have to explain to Miss Worsfold that he had lost an expensive piece of equipment. On the other hand, what counted for more – his life or the kite? The answer to that was obvious.

The moment he let go of the trapeze, the kite shot up in the air and then made a slow pirouette as it fell into the waves. Immediately Badger felt himself slow down and sink slowly into the water, his surfboard popping up beside him like a piece of flotsam. Then Mike was beside him, his boat engine idling. Badger felt the other boy's hands reach under his arms and, with surprising strength, haul him up into the boat.

"Now we'll pick up the surfboard and the kite," said Mike. "Then we can get back to the beach."

Mike proved to be a real expert. He soon had the surfboard in the boat, and after that it was only a matter of a minute or two before he had retrieved the kite.

Badger was exhausted.

"Don't try to talk," said Mike. "Just get your breath back. You'll be fine."

Mike turned the boat round and headed at full speed for the reef, now far in front of them.

"It was a good thing I was out here fishing," he said. "Otherwise you could have been half way to Cuba by now."

Badger ignored the advice not to talk. "You saved my life," he said.

Mike laughed. "I'm sure that somebody else would have rescued you."

"No," said Badger. "There's nobody else around – look. You really did save my life."

The other boy shrugged. "That's what happens at sea," he said. "If I saved your life, then somebody will probably save mine one of these days. We look after one another at sea, don't we?"

They did not take long to arrive at the beach.

"Hello, Badger," said Miss Worsfold, noticing that he looked shaken. "Is everything all right?"

Badger was about to tell her what had happened

Sharks tend not to come inside a reef: so you are usually safe if you stay there.

It suddenly dawned on Badger that he might die. *This is happening to me*, he thought. *This is not something I'm watching in a movie; this is real ...*

Mike turned the boat round and headed at full speed for the reef, now far in front of them ...

when Mike replied. "It's all fine, Miss," he said. "I was out there and we decided to come back in together." There was no mention of the danger that Badger had been in. But what Mike had said was, strictly speaking, true – he had been out there and yes, they had decided to come back in together.

Badger looked at his new friend with double gratitude. Not only had Mike saved his life, but he had saved him from looking foolish in front of everybody.

"If you want to go back to the *Tobermory* now," Miss Worsfold said to Badger, "then perhaps your friend will take you in his boat. You're such a natural kitesurfer there's no point in your staying for the rest of the lesson."

Badger thought this was a good idea. "And could I show Mike round the ship?" he said.

"I don't see why not," said Miss Worsfold. "And see if Cook can rustle up a doughnut or two for you. You've earned it with all that energetic activity."

The two boys left in Mike's boat.

"Thanks again," said Badger as they drew away from the beach. "Thanks for making me not look stupid in front of everybody."

Mike said nothing, but he smiled. He liked Badger. He liked what he had seen of Miss Worsfold. He liked everything about the *Tobermory*. *Oh, if only* … He stopped himself. There was no point in thinking about things that could never be. You have to live your life in the here and now, making do with what you have. You can dream, of course, but you have to remember that dreams are nothing more than that.

"Can we go back to my place first?" he asked Badger. "These fish have to go in the freezer."

He pointed to a box of fish – the day's catch – on the floor of the boat. In the excitement of the rescue, Badger had not seen it.

"Of course," said Badger. "I'll help you."

Mike grinned at him. "Smelly work," he warned.

"I don't mind," said Badger. He would do anything for the boy who had just saved his life.

They beached Mike's boat on the strip of sand directly outside the Wood family house. Badger helped to drag it up so that it would be out of the reach of the high tide, and watched as Mike secured it to the trunk of a fallen palm tree. Then Badger carried the oars while Mike lugged the fish box up the path that led to the house.

Mike's mother was at the door to greet them. She was a friendly woman whose face showed lines brought about by hard work and the burden of a thousand cares. Standing behind her was Mike's sister, who looked as if she was a year or two younger than her brother.

"This is my mother," said Mike. "And this is my sister, Ellie."

"Well, well," said Mike's mother as she shook hands with Badger. "You must be off that big sailing ship that's come in. Welcome to our house, young man."

Mike led Badger into the kitchen, where he emptied the fish box into a large white basin. They had been followed in by his mother, who inspected the fish, turning them over to check that they were in good condition.

"A nice catch," said Mrs Wood. "I'll clean them for the freezer. You go and chat to your friend. Give him a soda from the fridge."

Mike took Badger to his room. "This is where I sleep," he said. "That's my wardrobe over there and that's my table."

Badger noticed a stamp album on the table, with a pile of unsorted old stamps beside it.

"That's my hobby," said Mike. "I buy old stamps by the hundred – they cost hardly anything. Then I sort them out and stick them in the album."

Badger asked whether he could look at the album. Opening it at random, he flicked through pages filled with old stamps, filed away under the name of the country that had issued them: Uruguay, Vanuatu, Venezuela, Virgin Islands …

Badger turned to Mike. "All those places," he said. "Have you been to any of them?"

Mike shook his head. "I've never been anywhere. I hope one day I will get to go somewhere – who knows?"

Mike closed the album. "Have you always fished?"

"Yes," said Mike. "My dad was a fisherman too, and my granddad."

Badger noticed Mike had said *was* and wondered what had happened to his father, but did not want to ask directly. Mike, though, guessed what he was thinking.

"My dad's still alive," he said. "Or at least I hope he is."

Badger was puzzled. "How come you don't know for sure?"

Mike gestured to a chair and asked Badger to sit down. "I'll tell you the whole story," he said. "It begins when I was about ten, I suppose, which is three years ago. I'm thirteen now."

"Me too," said Badger, adding, "Just."

Mike started his story. "My dad had a good boat – one that could go far out to sea where the larger fish are – marlin, tuna and so on. I used to go out with him sometimes, but most of the time he went with a friend, a man called Sammy Williams. Well, once they decided to go all the way down to Dominica – that's an island south of us, about eighty miles away. They had heard there were big tuna down there and they thought they'd try their luck.

"Well, they caught plenty of fish and put them on ice and then anchored in a bay near a place called Indian River. They were planning to spend the night there before heading back up to Antigua. Uncle Sammy – I've always called him that – stayed on the boat that evening while my dad went to have a beer at one of the harbour bars. He never came back. Uncle Sammy waited and waited for him, and when there was no sign of him the next morning he went ashore to ask around. There were only two bars nearby and he asked in both of them. He found out my dad had been in one of them, and that he had gone off with two men. That was the last anyone saw of him."

"So he just disappeared?"

"Yes. Completely disappeared. Uncle Sammy went to the police and reported him missing. They said they'd look for him, but they had no idea what might have happened. They suggested that he should go the hospital to see if he had been brought in injured. He did that, but again there was no sign of my dad.

"Uncle Sammy sold the tuna in Dominica so he could stay and search further. He ended up staying two weeks, but found nothing – not a single trace. It was as if he had vanished into thin air."

Badger shook his head. "What a horrible thing," he said.

"Yes. Nobody knew what to think and we were all

very upset. We wondered whether he had had some terrible accident, or had even fallen into the water and drowned on his way back from the bar. But then we heard something that made us think differently. Apparently two other people had disappeared in very similar circumstances around the same time there. Nobody ever found out what had happened to them."

Badger was silent for a while. He couldn't imagine how awful it must be for someone to go missing in such circumstances. One of the hardest things must be simply not to know; you must think about it every single day, wondering what had happened, wondering whether you still had a father.

Mike stood up. "I'm sorry," he said. "I shouldn't go on about it. Other people aren't all that interested. They have their own problems to worry about."

"No," said Badger. "I'm sorry that it's such a sad story, but I'm glad you told me."

"Oh well," said Mike, trying to look more cheerful. "You said you'd show me the *Tobermory*. I'm ready now – can we go?"

Badger said goodbye to Mike's mother and thanked her for the soda. Then the two boys pushed the boat out into the waves once more and set off for the ship on the other side of the bay. Badger was silent all the way across – he was thinking of what it would be like to be Mike.

CHAPTER 11

Mike joins up

Unknown to Badger, somebody had been watching earlier as he surfed through the gap in the reef out into the open sea. It had not been Miss Worsfold or anybody else on the beach – they were too busy with their class to pay attention to what was going on elsewhere. But Captain Macbeth had not been too busy. He was standing on the deck of the *Tobermory*, looking through his binoculars at the ships anchored on the other side of the bay. He was not looking for anything in particular – sailors are often just interested in how other ships are rigged or the state of their paintwork, or some such detail. But as he scanned the bay, he noticed Badger on his surfboard and watched him for a few moments to see how he was getting on.

The Captain was impressed with Badger's speed and with his ability to keep the kite up high and full of wind. But then, as he saw him clear the reef, his admiration suddenly turned to concern. He wondered how Badger was going to cope with the much bigger waves, and within seconds he realised that even if Badger was not yet in serious trouble, he soon would be. And that meant a rescue mission.

But just as he was about to shout out an order to prepare the *Tobermory's* high-powered rescue boat he noticed that help was already at hand in the form of a small boat racing through the water towards Badger. Captain Macbeth smiled as he saw how quickly and efficiently the rescue was carried out, though even with his binoculars, he was too far away to see exactly who it was who had come to Badger's aid.

"Whoever it is knows what they're doing," he muttered to himself. It was easy for somebody like the Captain, with his years of experience, to spot people who really knew the sea.

So when Mike tied up his boat and climbed up the ladder with Badger, Captain Macbeth realised it must have been Mike who had come to Badger's rescue. He called the two boys across to speak to him.

"That's the Captain," Badger whispered to Mike. "He wants to speak to us."

Mike looked concerned. "Maybe I shouldn't be here," he said. "I don't want to get you into trouble."

"I won't get into trouble," said Badger. "We're allowed to show people round when we're at anchor."

They walked towards to the stern, where the Captain was standing. Captain Macbeth broke into a broad smile. "Oh, it's you," he said, addressing Mike. "You're the boy who took us over to see old Tommy."

"I was hoping to show Mike the ship," said Badger. "Is that all right, sir?"

The Captain nodded. "Of course it's all right, Tomkins, especially after your kitesurfing adventure."

Badger looked surprised. "You saw me …" he began.

The Captain cut him short. "I was watching," he said, gesturing to the binoculars hung round his neck. "I saw you go shooting out through the reef. And I was just about to launch the rescue boat when I saw Mike here head over towards you."

"I didn't know it would be so rough out there," said Badger, looking rather ashamed.

"Well, you've learned a lesson," said the Captain. "And I'm sure you won't do that again in a hurry."

Badger nodded. "I won't, Captain. I promise I won't."

The Captain made it clear that he was not angry – far from it, in fact. He was also impressed with what Mike had done and wanted to thank him.

"Your quick action saved the day," he said to Mike. "I could tell that you knew what you were doing."

Mike looked away modestly.

But the Captain was not going to leave it at that. "I shall write a note to Captain Tommy and tell him about it," he said. "He'll be mighty proud of you, I imagine."

"Thank you, sir," said Mike. "You don't need to do that, but thank you anyway."

After the Captain had given them a nod to show that they were dismissed, Badger took his friend off to climb up to the crow's nest. This was the small platform, right up at the top of the main mast, where the ship's lookout would perch and look far out over the sea in every direction.

Mike was a quick climber, and he also had a head for heights.

"I sometimes feel a bit dizzy up here," confessed Badger. "I look down and see how far it is to the deck below, and then I begin to think about what would happen if I slipped or let go."

"Don't," said Mike with a smile. "Never think of that. Never look down."

"I know," said Badger. "But it's hard."

They made their way back down to the deck, and Badger then took Mike to show him his cabin.

"This is where I sleep," he said. "This is my hammock over here, and that one over there is my friend Ben's."

"Where's he now?" asked Mike.

"He's doing his activity," said Badger. "Everybody has to do an activity during the afternoon. Ben's gone snorkelling."

Mike liked the word *activity*. "I'd like to have an activity," he said.

"But you've got one," said Badger. "Fishing."

"That's different," said Mike. "That's work."

As Mike looked around the cabin, Badger noticed that his expression had changed. When they had first come on board, Mike had looked excited and full of anticipation. Now he felt that his new friend was feeling sad.

'Are you okay?" he asked.

Mike nodded. "I'm fine," he said. "It's just … it's just …" He faltered. It seemed that he was having difficulty finding the right words for his feelings.

Badger waited. "Have you ever slept in a hammock?" he asked.

Mike shook his head. "It looks great," he said. "I'd like to try it one day.'

Badger opened the locker beside his bed. "I've got some chocolate," he said. "Would you like some?"

Mike took a couple of squares from the bar offered to him before passing it back to Badger, who also helped himself before wrapping it up again and replacing it in the locker.

And it was while he was doing this that the idea came to him. It was one of those ideas that arrives uninvited, one of those ideas so unexpected that it stops you in your tracks.

Of course what happens next is that you think: *impossible*. Then after that you begin to list the reasons why the idea will not work. And then, as often as not, you sigh and say to yourself, *It would have been such a wonderful thing to do – if only I had been able to do it.* And then you go back to what you were thinking about before – and that is the end of your brilliant idea. Except sometimes …

What Badger did next was to surprise him when he thought about it later.

"Do you mind if I leave you here for a few minutes?" he said. "I've got to go and see Mr Rigger."

Mike assured him that he did not mind. There was an old copy of a sailing magazine that Badger had on his shelf and he could leaf through that while he was waiting. "Take your time," said Mike. "I'll be all right."

Badger left the cabin and made his way along the passageway. The ship seemed deserted, with everybody busy with their afternoon activities, but Badger had an idea that he would find Mr Rigger in the staffroom. He knew this was where Mr Rigger liked to spend his spare time reading books about the famous sailor Horatio Hornblower. And sure enough, when he entered the staffroom, there was Mr Rigger, sprawled out on a chair, a Hornblower book in his hands.

"It's all very exciting," said Mr Rigger, looking up from his book. "Hornblower is in a real spot, I can tell you."

Badger cleared his throat. "I need my phone," he said.

Now it was a very strict rule that at the beginning of each trip all phones were handed over to Mr Rigger to be locked away for the duration of the voyage. "You don't need to talk to people all the time," the Captain had explained many times before. "And the whole point about going off to sea is to develop self-reliance. You can't be self-reliant if you're able to dial a number and ask somebody at the other end what to do, or check the internet."

There was another reason, and the Captain explained that too. "Safety," he had said. "If you're talking on the phone, you can't do your job, and accidents can happen. We almost had a terrible disaster before we introduced this rule." Everybody knew what he was talking about: on one occasion a member of the school had almost landed the ship on the rocks because he had been talking on his phone while he was at the helm.

It was a hard rule for some, as there were people who were addicted to their phones, but even they began to realise how much better life could be if they were not on the phone or checking their messages all the time.

"Your phone?" said Mr Rigger, his moustache beginning to bristle. "You know we can only allow that in very special circumstances."

Badger said that he thought these might be just such circumstances.

"But why?" asked Mr Rigger. "You can't just say

this is a special case – you have to tell me why."

Badger was ready to take the teacher into to his confidence. He liked Mr Rigger – everybody did – and knew he could trust him. Taking a deep breath, he began to tell Mr Rigger about Mike rescuing him. "So he saved my life," he said at the end.

Mr Rigger looked impressed. "You were very lucky he was around," he said. "But what's this got to do with needing your phone?"

Badger explained, telling Mr Rigger about the disappearance of Mike's father and how Mike had had to leave school to help support his family. Mr Rigger listened intently, nodding now and then to show he was following. At the end, he thought for a while before he spoke.

"Do you really think your parents would say yes?" Mr Rigger asked. "We'd like not to have to charge very much for a place on the *Tobermory*, but it's very expensive to run a ship like this, you know. There are some special funds for scholarships, of course, but the last one went to Tanya and there's nothing available at the moment, I'm afraid."

Badger assured him that he did know that it cost a lot. "But my parents have got heaps of money, Mr Rigger. They could afford this without even noticing."

"Very well," said Mr Rigger. "But what about this boy Mike? How do you know he wants to join the school?"

Badger told Mr Rigger about some of the remarks Mike had made earlier. "I know he'd love to join us," he said.

"But his mother is here, you say," said Mr Rigger. "And he has a fishing boat. Who's going to catch the fish to keep the family going?"

"His mother has another job," said Badger. "Selling fish is only part-time for her, and if Mike were on the *Tobermory* then they wouldn't need so much money anyway."

"I suppose so," said Mr Rigger. He seemed to think for a while and then continued, "All right, Badger, I think you've made out a very good case. But how do you know that the Captain will be able to fit him in?"

"The Captain likes him," said Badger. "I bet he'll find a place."

"You're probably right," said Mr Rigger. "Don't tell him I said this, but Captain Macbeth has a soft heart. He's one of the kindest men I know."

"Then he'll say yes?" Badger asked.

"Possibly," answered Mr Rigger. "But first things first. You make that call – and we needn't even bother to get your phone out of the storeroom. Use mine. I'm allowed to carry one for emergencies."

Mr Rigger extracted his phone from his pocket and handed it to Badger. His heart beating loudly, Badger dialled his father's number.

Far away in New York, a telephone rang. And then

a voice snapped, "Tomkins, Tomkins and Postle-thwaite. Whom do you wish to speak to?"

"My dad," blurted out Badger.

There was a slight delay before the voice answered. "Arch Tomkins the Third?" asked the voice.

"That's him," said Badger. "That's my dad."

"I'll see," said the voice. "Hold the line, please."

Badger closed his eyes. He knew how difficult it was to get in touch with his father, and he hoped it would be easier today.

The voice returned. "Mr Tomkins is very busy. Can he call you back?"

"I need to speak to him right now," said Badger. "Tell him it's really important."

Once again there was a delay, and then Badger heard his father on the line. "Badger, son? Is every-thing all right?"

"It's fine, Dad."

The relief was clear. "Good, in that case can I call you back some other time? I've got this big project on at the moment and the office is full of people."

"No, Dad," Badger said firmly. "This is important. I want to ask you a question."

"Sure," said his father, "But make it a short one, please."

Badger seized the opportunity; he had his father's attention at last. "If somebody saved my life," he began, "would you be grateful to him?"

"Saved your life? Of course I'd be grateful. I'd be *very* grateful." And then, after a short pause, "You are okay, aren't you? You did say you were all right."

"I'm fine, Dad. But I almost wasn't." Trying to be concise so as not to waste his father's time, Badger related the story of his rescue. At the end he said, "Mike – the boy who saved me – would love to be on this ship, but his family don't have the money. Can you pay his fees, Dad? As a thank you for saving my life?"

There, he thought. *I've asked the question, and now, I suppose, I'll hear the answer: No.* But that was not what happened.

"Sure, I'll pay the fees," came the reply. "And more than that: I'll give him pocket money too."

Badger was so astonished – and overjoyed – that it took him a little while to collect his thoughts.

"You still there, Badger?" asked his father.

"Yes, Dad, I'm here. And thank you so much. Thanks for being the kindest dad in … in … in New York."

There was a chuckle at his father's end of the line. "Oh, I don't know about that, but thanks anyway. May I speak to one of the teachers? I'll have to talk to someone about all this."

Badger handed the phone over to Mr Rigger, who had been listening to the conversation with growing pleasure and now discussed some details with Badger's father.

After the call was ended, Mr Rigger turned to Badger. "Now we'll need to go and ask the Captain. We can't tell Mike before we know he has a place."

As Badger had predicted, the Captain required no persuading. "That boy's a born sailor," he said. "It'll be a privilege to have him on board."

At the Captain's suggestion, Badger went off to fetch Mike from his cabin.

"The Captain wants to speak to you," he told him.

Mike looked worried. "What have I done?" he said.

"Oh, you're not in trouble," Badger reassured him. "In fact, quite the opposite. He just wants to ask you some questions."

"What do you mean?" Mike asked.

"You'll find out soon enough," said Badger. "But we can't keep him waiting. Come along with me."

Mike's interview in the Captain's cabin didn't take long. He was asked a few questions about his education up to that point and he was then quizzed by Mr Rigger about his knowledge of tides and winds. Finally, the Captain reached out to shake his hand, announcing, "You're in.'

"In what?" asked Mike, looking puzzled.

"You have a place on the *Tobermory*, paid for by a generous person. Do you think your mother will let you accept it?"

Mike knew he would not have to wait for an

answer: she had always wanted him to continue his education, but had been unable to afford it. He knew she would be pleased.

"You go and ask her then," said the Captain. "Just to be sure."

"I know she'll say yes," said Mike, his voice brimming with excitement and pleasure. "And when can I start, sir?"

The Captain shrugged. "Tomorrow morning, I'd say. That'll give you time to pack."

"Which deck will he be on, sir?" asked Badger.

The Captain looked at a list on his desk. "It'll have to be Upper Deck," he said. "There's a space in one of their cabins."

Badger's heart sank. Upper Deck was the last place he wanted Mike to be, as that was where William Edward Hardtack was Head Prefect. But there was worse to come.

"You'll be sharing a cabin with …" The Captain consulted his list again. "You'll be sharing with a boy called Maximilian Flubber."

Badger's heart sank even further, but he didn't want to spoil things for Mike. "That's great," he said, trying to sound enthusiastic. "That's just great."

There are times when you use words in such a way as to convey the opposite of what they really mean. And this was one of them.

The old sea-chest

They spent another two days in Green Island Bay. There were more kitesurfing classes, more diving instruction from Matron, and Mr Rigger held scuba-diving lessons. Ben jumped at the chance of learning how to use scuba equipment. Badger signed up for this too, and so did Mike, who despite living by the sea, had never been able to afford the costly equipment you need to breathe underwater. Once Mr Rigger had taught them the basics, they were able to descend to the sea bed on equal terms with the fish and turtles that lived there. From down below they looked up to see the hulls of the boats floating above them.

Fee and Poppy concentrated on diving lessons with Matron. At first they dived from a floating platform which was moored beside the *Tobermory*, then gradually they learned how to do higher and more complex dives from high up on the mast. Matron was a brilliant teacher, and they were soon doing swallow dives, half turns, corkscrews and even somersaults in mid-air.

"Good work, girls," shouted Matron as they surfaced. "But remember to keep your ankles together. Keep them together and you can't go wrong."

Mike settled in quickly. He loved everything about the *Tobermory* and he was a quick learner too. There was a small library on the ship, the shelves of which were lined with books about the sea. Mike spent a lot of time there, his nose buried in a book, absorbing all sorts of things he hadn't had the chance to learn before.

Of course, there were some things he knew already, as Captain Tommy had given him some valuable lessons. One of these was how to use flags to send signals. This is not easy, as you have to remember what each of the signalling flags means. There are special flags for whole messages – such as one that says *I am not in control of my vessel*. There is also one that says *I am about to leave port*, and a flag you can fly when there is a diver down below. But every flag, when used in conjunction with others, also represents a different letter of the alphabet. So by stringing flags one after the other, you can send any message you like. You can say *Happy Birthday*, for instance, or *Please send me more doughnuts, in particular ones with lots of jam inside* – if it is somebody's birthday on another ship or if you really need doughnuts. Of course, a long message will take a lot of flags and keep you busy for some time, so you should avoid sending messages like the one about doughnuts. And there is always a possibility that the person receiving the message might not see the flags properly, and might misread what you are trying to say. So *Please send me more doughnuts, in particular ones with lots of jam inside* might be read as *Please send me no more nuts – we have lots of jam inside*. That would lead to a lot of head-scratching and puzzlement. "No more nuts?" people would say. "What on earth do they mean by that? And why are they telling us they have lots of jam on board?'

Mike's mother knew how to read signalling flags, so he was able to send a message to her several times a day. Raising the flags on a special line tied to a high spar, he sent this message to his mother: HAVING A GREAT TIME, MA! VERY HAPPY! And from way over on the far shore, he was able to make out flags being raised in reply: GLAD TO HEAR THAT, BUT REMEMBER TO WEAR CLEAN SOCKS EVERY DAY. LOVE, MA.

Ben and Badger introduced Mike to all their friends, and everybody liked him immediately. Mr Rigger took a particular shine to Mike because he saw in him the makings of a really good sailor. He lent him a book on knots, although he was impressed with just how many knots Mike knew already.

"You'd win the knot competition hands down," said Ben, "if only there weren't certain people who are prepared to cheat."

He was talking about Hardtack, of course, and his two unpleasant lieutenants. Mike now knew all about them because he had already heard them sniggering about him at the table during dinner one evening.

"I saw him sending signals to his mum," Geoffrey Shark had said. "Poor little boy is probably homesick! Needs his mother to tuck him in at night!"

"Probably still scared of the dark," William Edward Hardtack had sneered. "Flubby, you share with him. Do you have to leave the light on at night? Got a night-light for baby?"

Flubber had not replied, as he knew that Mike could hear and Flubber would never say anything mean about another person if he thought that person would hear it. He would wait to say it when his back was turned – then he would be every bit as spiteful as Hardtack or Shark.

Mike was strong, though. He had encountered people like this before and had not let them intimidate him. At the same time, it was hurtful to hear himself being described by Shark as "some riff-raff the Captain's taken on. Some nobody from a tiny little island. Some nothing fisher-boy with no more than two cents to his name."

"Don't worry about those guys," Ben told him. "Nobody listens to them – I promise you. We just ignore it."

"But they called me riff-raff," said Mike. "I don't like that at all."

"Forget it," advised Ben. "If anybody's riff-raff, it's them."

"And they laugh at me because I'm poor," Mike went on. "I can't help that. My dad went missing, you see …"

"I've heard what happened," said Ben. "Badger told me. You've had very bad luck. But, as I say, just ignore them. And so what if Hardtack's dad owns big hotels somewhere? I've heard that he got the money to buy them from some scam he was running. He's lucky the police haven't arrested him by now."

The support of people like Ben and Badger helped Mike a great deal, but it still was not easy feeling the hostility of that unpleasant trio. Bullies are best ignored – Mike knew that – but it is sometimes hard to do that when you are their victim.

On the night before they were due to leave Green Island Bay, word came that the Captain wanted to see those people who had accompanied him on his visit to Captain Tommy. That was Poppy and Fee, Ben and Badger, Thomas and, of course, Mike. So the six of them gathered after dinner and Poppy knocked loudly on the Captain's door. "He likes you to knock firmly," she explained to Mike. "If you knock too softly he pretends he can't hear so you have to knock louder. He says it's something to do with confidence."

From inside the cabin they heard the Captain's voice telling them to come in. Once they were lined up smartly in front of his desk, he told them to stand at ease.

"That old sea-chest," he said, looking up from his papers. "I promised you'd be able to sort through Captain Tommy's things. Are you still keen to do that?"

Poppy spoke for them all. "Definitely, Captain."

"Well, in that case," he continued, "the chest is over there in the corner. Go and have a look and we'll see what's inside."

Holding her breath with excitement, Poppy prised open the lid.

The hinges were stiff with rust, and she needed help. Mike pulled on one side and Badger on the other, and very slowly they opened the chest completely.

If they had been expecting treasure, then they were in for a disappointment. But since none of them really know what to expect, they did not feel let down when they saw what the chest contained.

The Captain was looking over their shoulders.

Matron was a brilliant teacher, and they were soon doing swallow dives, half turns, corkscrews and even somersaults in mid-air ...

So by stringing flags one after the other, you can send any message you like.

Holding her breath with excitement, Poppy prised open the lid ...

"Well, well," he said, as he surveyed the contents. "Exactly what I'd expected."

Badger picked up a small box made of highly polished wood. "What's in here, Captain?" he asked.

"I'd say it's a sextant," answered the Captain. "But why don't you open it and find out?"

Badger unhooked a small brass latch on the side of the box and opened up the lid. The Captain was right: within the box, nestling on a layer of baize cloth, was a sextant, complete with its tiny viewing mirrors and lens.

"You all know what this is for, I assume," said the Captain. "Has everybody used one?"

Hands went up, but not every hand. Mike had never used a sextant, and neither had Ben.

"I'll show you tomorrow," said the Captain. "We'll have to wait until noon. At twelve o'clock on the dot we can use this to take a sighting of the sun that'll show us exactly where we are on the ocean."

The sextant was replaced in its box and they moved in to the next item. This was an old compass in a cracked leather case. "Now I'm sure everybody will have used one of these," said the Captain.

The compass had been made a long time ago, and its rose – the dial on which the degrees were inscribed – had been painted by hand. Poppy held it flat for a few moments and watched the tiny needle quiver, spin round, and settle in position.

"That's north," she said. "And that's south. See — it still works perfectly."

Mike picked up the next item, which was the tooth of some creature, on which somebody had scratched a picture of a boat in full sail. That was on one side – on the other was a picture of a sailor with a beard looking through a telescope.

"Anybody know what that is?" asked the Captain.

"The tooth of a whale?" suggested Poppy.

"Right first time," said the Captain. "It's the tooth of a sperm whale, I'd say. And some sailor way back spent a lot of time engraving those drawings on it. We call these things scrimshaw."

They handed round the tooth.

"Poor whale," said Fee.

The Captain nodded. "It was a cruel business,

176

whale hunting. Those poor creatures were hunted to the edge of extinction. Fortunately, it stopped – apart from one or two people who still do it."

They were silent for a moment, thinking of what it must be like to be a whale and to be pursued by whaling boats with their great harpoons.

"Horrible," said Poppy, shaking her head.

The Captain bent down to rummage in the items that remained. There was a box of pencils, an old cap, a bo'sun's whistle, and a watch. There was a set of sea clothes, still freshly pressed and not at all mouldy, and finally, under an oilskin-wrapped sailor's knife, was a large piece of folded paper.

"That looks like a chart," said the Captain, picking it up and beginning to unfold it.

"Ah yes," he said. "I believe that's exactly what it is."

They all pored over the chart as the Captain spread it out on the floor.

"It looks like an island," said Badger. "Look – there's a harbour and there's a river over there."

"And some hills," said Ben, pointing to a place behind the harbour.

"And a volcano," added Mike, drawing their attention to a triangular shape near the centre of the map. "Those squiggles look like smoke coming from the crater. There are lots of volcanos in the Caribbean, you know."

"Where do you think it is?" asked Poppy.

The Captain shook his head. "I have no idea," he said. "It doesn't look like anywhere I know."

"It must be of somewhere around here," said Mike. "Captain Tommy always sailed in these waters."

"That's true," said the Captain, staring at one section of the chart. He put a finger on a section of sea near the island's shore. "Look at that. It shows a very rocky passage. There's plenty of detail – every rock's there."

"And that bit over there?" asked Fee, pointing to a place on a section marked *Beach*. "What's that?"

The Captain peered more closely. He drew in his breath. "Well, well," he began. "It's a long time since I've seen that on a chart."

"What is it?" pressed Ben.

"Quicksand," said the Captain. "It shows where there are sinking sands."

The Captain spoke in a hushed voice, and it seemed to all of them that there was a note of fear in his tone. This was unusual – he was normally confident and frightened of nothing, but now he seemed worried.

"What's quicksand?" asked Badger.

Thomas Seagrape knew the answer to that. "Sands that are full of water – a bit like custard," he said, quite cheerfully. "But if you walk over them you'll sink. Gulp! Down you go."

The Captain spoke to him sharply. "It's no joke, Thomas," he said. "I've known people to have a very nasty time in sinking sands." He paused, remembering something painful. "People say they can suck you right down – they can't. But you can get badly stuck in them – right up to your chest. And then, if the tide comes in you would certainly drown. I had a friend who was stuck in sinking sands for ten hours once. He was lucky to get out alive."

Fee shivered. There were enough dangers at sea, she thought, without sinking sands being added to the list.

But then the Captain cheered up. "Still," he said, "let's not worry too much about that. I don't think these particular sinking sands are any danger to us: we don't even know where the island is."

Over the next half hour or so they busied themselves with tidying up and dusting the things they had found in the chest. Then the chest itself was given a thorough cleaning before its contents were neatly packed back inside. After that, the Captain dismissed them, and they returned to their cabins to get ready to set sail the following morning. Ben found himself thinking of the chart and the mysterious island it showed, but did not have time to dwell too long on the subject. Being at sea is like that – there is always something to do here and now.

Once lights were out, Ben and Badger chatted for

a while across their cabin, as they often did just before they dropped off to sleep. They had fifty miles or so of sea to cross the next day, and they were wondering what the waves would be like. The islands of the Caribbean can be windy, with the Trade Winds that blow right across the Atlantic from Africa. Those winds were blowing that night, and even in their cabin, well below deck, the boys could hear the sound of the wind in the rigging. Both were pleased that they were safely in their hammocks rather than up on deck on such a night.

"Quicksand," muttered Ben. "What would you do if you trod in quicksand, Badger?"

Badger did not reply immediately. Then a sleepy voice came from the other side of the cabin. "I'd try not to move. I think that if you struggle, it only makes it worse."

Ben thought about this. "You'd have to hope somebody would find you," he said.

"Yes," came the drowsy reply. "You'd have to …"

But there was nothing more. Badger had gone to sleep.

Ben smiled to himself. He did not mind if his friend went to sleep when he was talking to him. Perhaps it meant that he agreed with him …

The next morning at five, just when the first glimmers of light were appearing in the east but the sky directly above was still in darkness, the bell at the end of the passageway on each deck was given a resounding ring by Mr Rigger.

"Up, up up!" he shouted. "Everybody up! Weighing anchor in one hour, ladies and gentlemen!'

Everyone knew that when Mr Rigger used the words *ladies and gentlemen* he meant business, and you had to snap to. You had to get out of your hammock the moment you heard him and run, not walk, to the shower. You wouldn't have more than ten minutes to wash and get your clothes on before rushing to the mess for breakfast. After that, it was back down below to clean your teeth and check your lifejacket was at hand before making your way up on deck to report for duty.

Nobody minded the rush that day, of course, as they remembered this was the day they were due to sail from Antigua to an island to the south. They had been told the name of this island, but everybody seemed to have trouble pronouncing it.

"What's this place called again?" Tanya asked Poppy. "G … something or other. I really don't know how to say it – do you?"

Poppy had been practising. "This is how you say it: GWAR DE LOOP. You spell it GUADE-LOUPE, but you say it the way I've just said."

"GWAR DE LOOOP," said Tanya, struggling to get her mouth round the strange sounds.

"They speak French there," said Poppy. "So if we go ashore …"

"Which we will be doing," said Fee. "I heard the Captain saying we'd be able to."

"Well, when we do," said Poppy, "there'll be really nice bread and cakes because that's what you find wherever you hear French being spoken."

There were other things to look forward to.

"We're going to be anchoring near a place called Pigeon Island," Badger told Ben. "That's just off Guadeloupe, and it's a fantastic place for snorkelling."

"I can try out my new snorkel," said Ben.

"And I can use my new flippers," said Badger.

When the time came to weigh anchor, there wasn't a single person who did not feel the excitement. Even the ship seemed keen to start the journey, her sails filling with wind the moment they were unfurled. As they set off, the *Tobermory*'s bow throwing off white waves of sparkling water, all eyes were fixed on the horizon ahead. But their destination was still too far away to be seen, though they could make out, just visible in the distance, the island of Montserrat, with its great volcano reaching up into the clouds.

There was a lot to do. The sails had to be kept well-trimmed, set in just such a way as to make the best of the wind, and the deck had to be kept clear of ropes. These were neatly wound, ready for use but out of the way of people's feet. Then there were the normal tasks of keeping the ship in good order, the scrubbing and polishing and repairing that never seemed to stop.

They took it in turns to climb up to the crow's nest to keep a look-out for land, and it was Mike's good luck to be up there with Badger when they caught sight of Guadeloupe. At first it was not much more than a dark smudge, and Mike had to rub his eyes to make sure he was not imagining it.

"Is that it?" he asked Badger.

Badger had a small pair of binoculars, and he used these to look in the direction that Mike was pointing in.

"Yes, that's it," he said. "You saw it first. You call out."

"What do I say?" asked Mike.

Badger told him, and so Mike, cupping his hands to his mouth, shouted at the top of his lungs, "*Land ahoy!*"

That was the signal for people down below to rush to the bow to see if they could spot land. It was now time for Mike and Badger to climb back down to the deck, to allow others their turn in the crow's nest. As it happened, next in line were Geoffrey Shark and Maximilian Flubber. As they passed on the rope ladder, Shark sneered at Mike.

"Ignore him," whispered Badger.

"I'm trying," Mike whispered back. "But it's really hard. I'd like to give him a good push."

"No," said Badger. "That would only make it worse."

Back on deck, they went to chat to Thomas Seagrape, who was tidying up some ropes at the bottom of the mast. As they were talking to Thomas, they heard a shout from the crow's nest.

"It's a ship!" cried Geoffrey Shark from above. "That last call was a false alarm! It's a ship."

Badger caught his breath. "It looked like an island," he said. "I was sure it was Guadeloupe."

Mike looked down at the deck. "I was too," he muttered. He hated the thought that he had misled everybody, including the Captain.

Then somebody from the bow shouted out, "Yes, it's a ship. Look over there. It's just a large ship."

Now it was obvious that Mike had been wrong, as the shape of a ship could be made out quite clearly, steaming off towards Antigua.

"I'm going to go and apologise to the Captain," said Mike.

Badger said that he would apologise too. "I looked through my binoculars," he said. "I got it wrong too."

The Captain, who was at the helm, did not mind at all. "It's very easy to make that mistake," he said. "But perhaps next time you should just wait a few minutes until you're absolutely sure."

It was a gentle reproof, and Mike felt himself blushing with embarrassment as he walked away.

And it did not help when he heard a voice behind him say, "You need to get your eyes tested, you know. Maybe a pair of glasses will help."

Mike turned round. It was William Edward Hardtack.

"It looked like land," Mike said. "It really did."

Hardtack laughed. "Here's a guy who can't tell the difference between land and a ship," he sneered. "Well, here's something to help you remember. A ship moves, land doesn't. That's one difference. And here's another: a ship has a funnel coming out the top, or sails. Land doesn't. There – get it? Will that help you tell the difference in future?"

"Don't say anything," whispered Badger.

But his advice was too late. Goaded by these snide comments from Hardtack, Mike swung his fist and punched his tormentor right on the nose. Hardtack reeled back, clutching at his nose with both hands.

The Captain saw this. "You there!" he roared. "Stop that immediately and come over here."

Mike made his way to stand in front of the Captain.

"Now you listen to me, young man," said the Captain, his voice raised in anger. "I will not have any violence on my ship. Understand?"

Badger spoke up in his friend's defence. "Hardtack started it, sir. I heard him."

"You keep out of it, Tomkins," snapped the

Captain. And then, to Mike, he said, "Go to your cabin and stay there until I call for you. Understand?"

Looking the picture of misery, Mike nodded and went off. In the meantime, the Captain had summoned Hardtack over to his side and was examining the boy's nose.

"What did you say to him?" the Captain asked. "He said you started it."

Hardtack's jaw dropped. "But Captain, that's a lie," he protested. "I just said he was really good at climbing rope ladders. I was trying to be friendly."

The Captain looked at him. It was a severe look that seemed to say, *I don't believe that for one moment.* "I'm watching you, Hardtack," he said. "Just remember that."

An hour or so later, when the Captain had handed the wheel over to Mr Rigger, Badger was sent to bring Mike to the Captain's cabin. Once there, both boys were told to stand in front of the big oak desk.

"I'm very disappointed in you," the Captain said to Mike. He paused. "I'm prepared to believe that Hardtack asked for it, but whatever he said to you is no excuse for hitting him. Do you understand?"

"Sorry, sir," said Mike. "And yes, I understand."

The Captain turned to Badger. "And you, Tomkins, you should have stopped it before it started. You're meant to be showing this young man a good example."

Badger hung his head. He wished he had

managed to stop the fight, but it had started so quickly he was not sure that he would have been able to do anything.

The Captain shook his head. "You know that I can't let fighting go unpunished," he said. "So you'll both get one hour cleaning the heads. And you can do it while everyone else goes snorkelling at Pigeon Island. Do you understand?"

Badger nodded miserably. He had been looking forward to swimming among the clear blue water, and now he wouldn't be going.

"Dismissed," said the Captain, signalling for them to leave.

Outside, Mike said to Badger, "I'm really, really sorry I did that, Badger."

Badger shrugged. "Well, at least the Captain knew we were telling the truth. You could see that."

"Could you?" asked Mike.

"Yes," said Badger. "One hour of cleaning the heads is the very lightest punishment he could have given us. He knows what Hardtack's like, you see, but you went and punched him and that put you – put us both, I suppose – in the wrong…"

"I'm sorry," said Mike. "I really am, Badger."

Badger smiled bravely. "Well, no use crying over spilt milk – what's done is done." He sighed. "Well, at least I can show you how we clean the heads. We may as well get everything ready."

13

Bert Thorn makes an appearance

The crossing had gone more quickly than expected, as the winds had been strong. Of course, that meant that the waves were very large, but the *Tobermory* was used to rough seas and took them in her stride. Once they reached the island, though, the sea calmed down, and they sailed down the coast of Guadeloupe with scarcely a pitch or a roll.

Pigeon Island was a tiny island a short distance off the mainland. The sea bed around it was a sunken forest of coral, with thick columns rising up like tree trunks. All through the coral swam shoals of brightly coloured fish, hiding behind fronds of seaweed or darting out to catch some food. It was a paradise for divers and snorkellers, and after the *Tobermory* had anchored just about everybody changed into swimming costumes, donned masks and slipped into the clear blue water. Everybody except Mr Rigger, who stayed to look after the ship, Cook, who did not like swimming, and Badger and

Mike, who had their unpleasant cleaning task to do.

Mr Rigger looked as if he knew how they felt. "I'm sorry to hear what happened," he said, lowering his voice. "There's no excuse for punching somebody, but … well, let me put it this way – if I ever felt like punching anybody, then it would be …" He did not finish the sentence, but Badger and Mike knew exactly who he meant.

"Hardtack started it, Mr Rigger," said Badger.

Mr Rigger nodded. "One of these days he'll get what he deserves." He was about to say something else, but stopped himself.

A few minutes later, as they were busy filling buckets with water, Cook popped his head round the door of the boys' heads. "I heard you had a bit of trouble with a certain party," he said.

A certain party: this was a way of talking about Hardtack that made Badger smile. "I'm afraid so," said Badger, and then added, "That's why we're here and not out there snorkelling."

Cook shook his head. "It's a bad business when somebody who richly deserved a punch is out there swimming and the person who gave it to him is on board cleaning the heads." He shook his head again as he reached into a bag. "Still, I thought you might like some special doughnuts I made for you. Extra jam. Really delicious."

Cook extracted a large doughnut from the bag and

handed it to Mike. Then he took out another and passed it to Badger.

The two boys laid aside their mops.

"Thank you, Cook," said Badger. "They look terrific."

"Don't go punching anybody else, mind," warned Cook. "We can't have punching on this ship … no matter how much it's deserved." He leaned forward and whispered to Mike, "Tell me, young fellow, where did your fist collide with young Hardtack? Not that I'm saying you should have done it – oh, no, I'm not saying that – but where exactly did he get it?"

"On the nose," said Mike.

"Hah!" said Cook. "Very good! What a good place for somebody like that to be punched, not that I'm saying you should ever punch anybody – I'm not saying that. No, definitely not. Very bad. Very, very bad."

Cook went off chuckling, leaving the two boys to finish their doughnuts.

"That was good of Cook," said Mike, as he licked the last crumbs off his fingertips.

It was some hours before the others returned to the *Tobermory*. Alone on the deck, Badger and Mike watched morosely as the boats tied up at the bottom of the ship's ladder. They listened as people chatted excitedly about what they had seen, and tried not to look disappointed.

"Don't worry," said Badger. "There'll be plenty of chances to go snorkelling later on."

"I feel as if I've made a really bad start," said Mike. "More or less on my first day I go and punch somebody on the nose!"

Badger tried to comfort him. "Everybody gets into trouble now and then," he said. "I'm sure you won't be up in front of the Captain again for a long time."

"I hope not," said Mike.

Later that evening, the two boys had the chance to hear from the others about what they had seen on the reef. Even the nervous Angela Singh had enjoyed snorkelling and was sure she had seen a shark. But Poppy, who had been swimming next to her at the time, said that Angela was wrong and that her mask had simply distorted her vision and what she had seen was simply a long grey fish.

Because most people were tired after the journey from Antigua and the snorkelling expedition, dinner was served early. Afterwards they returned to their cabins for an evening of reading, writing postcards, or the simple mending tasks that sailors always seem to have to do: sewing rents in clothing, re-threading laces in deck shoes, or repairing the straps on life-jackets.

In their cabin, Ben told Badger about some of the sea creatures he had seen.

"There was a moray eel," he said. "I saw it looking at me from its hole in the rock."

Badger whistled. "You've got to be careful of those things," he said. "They have razor-sharp teeth, and if they get hold of you they don't let go. They can drown you if you're not careful."

Ben shuddered. "I didn't get too close," he said.

"Just as well," said Badger.

Ben said nothing. It was best not to think too much about narrow escapes, he thought, and he decided to talk about something else. "You know that chart in Captain Tommy's chest?" he began. "Why do you think he had it?"

Badger shrugged. "I suppose he might have used it some time. Mike said that he sailed all around these parts."

"But why would he have a chart of that island in particular?" pressed Ben. "And there's something else. When I was looking at it, I saw that someone had written something on the chart near the middle of the island: *This is where they might be*."

"Just that?" asked Badger.

"Yes," said Ben. "Who do you think *they* might be?"

Badger had no idea. Then he thought of something. "Some of these old charts were used by pirates. They marked where they buried the stuff they stole from ships – chests of gold and so on."

Ben considered this for a moment. "That's an interesting idea," he said, "but I don't think that's what this means. If it were treasure, surely it would say *This is where it might be*, not *they*. *They* sounds like people rather than a thing."

"But it could be things – plural," said Badger.

Ben agreed. "I don't think we'll ever know," he said at last. "And perhaps even Captain Tommy wouldn't be able to tell us, even if he was the person who wrote on the map. People write notes to themselves and then forget them. Haven't you done that, Badger? Haven't you ever thought of something and then forgotten all about it?"

Badger pretended to forget what they were talking about. "What was that you said?" he asked, and then laughed.

"Right," said the Captain to the whole school at muster the next morning. "We're staying here for a day or two, so those of you who want to go ashore can go. A boat will be organised by Mr Rigger."

This brought an excited murmur. Being at sea meant that people had nothing to spend their pocket money on, so a trip to the small harbour town would be a chance to do some shopping. Badger planned to renew supplies of his favourite chocolate bar; Fee had run out of shampoo and needed to stock up with more; and Poppy needed new batteries for her flashlight. Everybody, it seemed, needed something. Even Cook, who prided himself on never running out of anything, thought it would be useful to get fresh eggs and dispatched one of his assistants to buy some.

The friends all went ashore together. "I'll be back for you in two hours," Mr Rigger said cheerily as he set off from the quay to ferry across more students from the *Tobermory*.

While Poppy, Tanya, Angela and Fee went off to buy shampoo and batteries, Ben, Badger, Thomas and Mike went to a store that looked as if it might sell the sort of chocolate that Badger liked. When they had done that, they found their way to a café that sold fresh coconuts. These had their tops sliced off and straws inserted so the sweet coconut water could be drunk straight from the fruit.

It was delicious, and the boys had two each as they sat on stools in front of the counter. As they were drinking the coconut water, a man came in and made his way over.

"Good morning Mr Thorn," said the woman behind the counter. "Your usual coffee?"

Mike's eyes widened. "Did you hear that?" he whispered to Badger.

"Hear what?" asked Badger.

Mike nodded his head in the direction of the man's back. "She called him Mr Thorn," he said, his voice so low that even right next to him, Badger had difficulty in hearing.

Thorn? he thought. *Where have I heard that name*

Cook popped his head round the door. "I heard you had a bit of trouble with a certain party."

"There was a moray eel," Ben said. "I saw it looking at me from its hole in the rock."

These had their tops sliced off so the sweet coconut water could be drunk straight from the fruit.

before? And then he remembered: Bert Thorn was the pirate who had tried to board Captain Tommy's ship and whose own ship had been rammed by Captain Macbeth.

Keeping his voice as quiet as possible, Badger asked, "Is that *him*?"

Mike wasn't sure. "It could be," he said. "Thorn is quite an unusual name around here."

The man did not take long to drink his coffee. Turning round, he wiped the line of milk foam off his moustache and made his way out, barely sparing the boys a glance. They had a chance to see his face, though, and they did not like what they saw. All the way down one cheek was a long scar that looked as if it had been made by the swipe of a knife, and his thick bushy eyebrows lent an angry look to what was already a rather frightening face.

Once the stranger had gone, Badger had an idea. "I'm going to ask," he muttered as he rose to his feet.

"Ask what?" said Ben.

"About him. About Mr Thorn.'

"I'd like to pay for our coconuts," Badger said to the woman behind the counter, a couple of banknotes at the ready.

The woman smiled and added up the bill:

"I was wondering about Mr Thorn," said Badger, trying to sound as casual as possible. "That is Bert Thorn, isn't it?"

"That's Bert," said the woman. "Do you boys know him?"

Badger shook his head. "Not personally," he said.

"He uses another name these days," said the woman. "I still call him Mr Thorn but most people call him Mr Butterfield now. I think he …" She lowered her voice. "I think he might have been in a bit of trouble in the past, and that's why he changed his name."

Badger said that he thought most people would have forgotten about that. "I heard something about that," he said. "But it was a long time ago."

"Yes," said the woman. "He's just bought himself a new boat, the *Barracuda*, I think it's called. It's over there in the harbour – you might have seen it."

"I'll look out for it," said Badger.

The woman smiled again. "In fact, he's looking for crew. I know he wants a couple of cabin boys … Any of you fellows interested? I wouldn't sign up myself, mind you," she continued. "Not on Bert Thorn's boat. I don't like where he goes."

Badger was interested. "Oh? Where's that?"

The woman hesitated. She looked about her as if to make sure there was nobody else within earshot. "He goes out to a place called Shark Island," she said. "Backwards and forwards, picking things up and bringing them back here." She gave a shudder. "I don't fancy going anywhere near Shark Island – not me."

Badger tried to sound casual. "Shark Island?" he said. "I don't think I've heard of it. Where is it?'

The woman did not answer immediately, and seemed to think carefully before responding. "You don't want to know where Shark Island is. There's been a lot of talk about that place."

Badger raised an eyebrow. "Oh? Such as?"

The woman lowered her voice. "A few people have gone missing round here," she said. "Like they've vanished into thin air. It's said that they might have ended up on Shark Island."

Badger noticed that when she said this, Mike stiffened.

The woman looked at her watch. "I must get on with my work," she said.

Badger nodded. "We have to get back to our ship. Thanks for the coconuts."

Once outside, the others gathered round Badger.

"Well," said Thomas, "what do you make of that?"

The question was addressed to Badger, but it was Mike who answered.

"I think we need to investigate," he said. "The woman said that people had gone missing, didn't she?"

Badger nodded. He remembered the story Mike had told him about his father's disappearance. Could it be that Bert Thorn and Shark Island were somehow connected with that?

Mike had clearly made up his mind. "I want to speak to the Captain," he said, "and tell him about everything we've found out today."

"All right," said Badger. "Although let me warn you about one thing."

"What's that?" asked Mike.

"Don't expect adults to see things quite the way we see them," answered Badger. "Sometimes they do, but other times they don't. So …"

Ben completed the sentence for him: "So don't build up your hopes too much."

Mike listened, but he was not going to be put off. For the first time in three years he saw a glimmer of light in the dark mystery of his father's disappearance. It was only a faint glimmer, but sometimes a glimmer can grow stronger and stronger until it becomes as clear and as strong as the midday sun …

Shortly afterwards they were all back on board the *Tobermory* again. At the top of the ladder, Matron was helping people back on board, checking names off against a list.

As she came to Mike's name, she looked up from her list.

"Oh yes, Wood. The Captain wanted to see you when you came back. Run along to his cabin right now, please."

Mike glanced at Badger. Was he in trouble again

– and so soon after the last time? As they walked away, Mike turned to his friend. "I haven't done anything," he said.

"Of course you haven't," Badger reassured him.

"Then why does he want to see me?"

Badger shrugged. "I don't know. It could be anything. Perhaps a message from home – something like that. I shouldn't worry, if I were you. I'll wait for you outside the Captain's cabin, though I'm sure it's nothing important."

For a full fifteen minutes Mike remained inside the Captain's cabin. When he came out, Badger knew immediately that something was seriously wrong. His friend was in tears.

CHAPTER 14

A false accusation

Thomas, Badger, Ben, Poppy, Fee, Tanya, Angela …
they were all there when Mike told them what had
happened in the Captain's cabin. And they were all
shocked.

"I had no idea why he wanted to see me," Mike
began. "But the moment I went in, I could tell that
it was something bad."

"You can always tell," said Angela. "If the Captain's
cross, his face looks like this." She put on an expression that looked just the way the Captain's did when
he was angry.

"So what happened, then?" pressed Poppy. "Did
he shout at you?"

Mike shook his head. "No, he didn't shout. His
voice was very quiet, as if he was trying to control it.
He said … he said …"

Mike faltered, and Badger stretched out to put an
arm on his shoulder. "Tell us in your own good time,"
he said. "Don't worry."

Mike took a deep breath. "No, it's all right," he said. "I can talk about it."

They waited a few moments while he composed himself.

"He said that there had been a theft," Mike continued. "He had gone to look for something in Captain Tommy's sea-chest and that when he opened it he saw that the sextant was missing, and the compass and chart had also gone."

Poppy gasped. "And he accused you of taking them?"

Mike nodded. "Yes. He said that somebody had reported seeing me carrying something into my cabin just before we went ashore."

"But you were with me," protested Badger.

"Yes," said Ben. "I saw the two of you together on deck. I can tell him that."

"Let Mike carry on," said Poppy. "So what happened next?"

"He told me that he went with Miss Worsfold to look in my cabin and they found the sextant and the compass in my locker."

"And the chart?" asked Ben.

Mike explained that they had failed to find the chart and that the Captain had accused him of hiding it somewhere else. "But I hadn't hidden anything," said Mike, his voice faltering again.

"Because you hadn't stolen anything," said Tanya.

"How could you have hidden something you didn't steal?"

"Exactly!" said Poppy.

None of them thought – even for one moment – that Mike would have stolen anything. None of them doubted that this was a complete set-up – that somebody else had taken the sextant and the compass and planted them in Mike's locker.

"I wonder who told the Captain they saw you," mused Poppy.

"Or who planted those things in your locker," added Tanya.

"No prizes for answering that," said Badger. "Flubber. He shares with Mike. It would have been the easiest thing for him to put them there."

"And then go and report that he had seen Mike carrying something," said Ben.

Poppy looked at Mike. "Did you tell him that somebody else must have done all that?" she asked.

Mike nodded.

"And did he listen?" asked Thomas.

"He listened," said Mike. "But I don't think he believed me. He just sat there looking at me while I tried to tell him I had nothing to do with it."

"And then?" prompted Badger.

"Then I was going to tell him about us seeing Bert Thorn today, but before I could he said that I should go back to my cabin and that he would want to see me again tomorrow morning."

They broke up, as they had to get ready for dinner. But before he left to go down to his cabin, Badger spoke quietly to Mike. "I'll go with you," he said. "I'll tell him you were with me. We'll get Ben to confirm that he saw us. He can't ignore the word of two people."

Mike thanked him, but from the way he looked, Badger could tell that his words had brought little comfort.

"Try and cheer up," Badger urged. "It'll all be sorted out."

But Mike said nothing.

The following morning at muster there was no sign of Mike. Mr Rigger was taking the roll, and called out Mike's name three times, but there was no reply. Then, after waiting for a minute or two, he asked the whole school, "Anybody seen Mike Wood?"

Nobody answered. Ben and Badger exchanged worried glances, but said nothing. Mike had been at dinner the previous evening, but they had not seen him since.

Mr Rigger walked over to where Maximilian Flubber was standing. "Flubber," he said. "You share with Wood, don't you? Have you seen him this morning?"

Flubber shook his head. "He wasn't in his

hammock when I woke up, sir. I thought he'd got up early."

"But you saw him last night?" asked Mr Rigger.

"Yes, he was in his hammock at lights-out."

"Did he say anything?" asked Mr Rigger.

"No," said Flubber. "We don't talk much."

Mr Rigger took a step back. Then he acted. "Search the ship!" he called out in as loud a voice as he could manage. "Everybody search your own deck. Look everywhere. Deck prefects, report back to me after you've completed the search."

If somebody goes missing at sea, a thorough search must be made immediately. If this brings no result, then the ship must be turned round and a much wider search carried out, in the hope that a bobbing head or a waving arm will be spotted somewhere in the water.

The search took almost half an hour, and when it was finished the deck prefects went back up to report.

"Anybody found anything?" asked Mr Rigger, sounding increasingly anxious.

There was a unanimous shaking of heads. Mike, it seemed, was no longer on board.

It was after Mr Rigger had gone down below to report to the Captain that Bartholomew Fitzhardy suddenly cried out: "One of the boats ... Look! One of the boats is missing."

Bartholomew was right. One of the liberty boats

on the starboard side had been let down into the water and was now no longer to be seen. The ropes by which it had been suspended were swinging loose from their blocks.

This could mean only one thing: Mike was no longer on board the *Tobermory*.

Badger looked thoughtful.

"I'm going to go and speak to the Captain," he said to Ben. "Are you going to come with me? You were there, after all."

"Where?" asked Ben.

"In the café," said Badger. "Because that's the key to it all. It's all about that, don't you see?"

Ben thought for a moment. "You mean ..."

"Yes. He'll have signed up as a cabin boy on Bert Thorn's ship. I'm sure of it."

Ben caught his breath. If things had looked bad earlier on, they looked a whole lot worse now. "I'll come with you," he said. "Let's go right now."

The Captain was deep in discussion with Mr Rigger when Ben and Badger entered his cabin after knocking loudly. He looked at them with irritation. "What is it?" he asked crossly. "Can't you see that Mr Rigger and I are busy? A boy is missing, you know …"

"We think we know where he is," blurted out Badger.

"Yes," said Ben, supporting his friend. "We were in a café, you see, and …"

The Captain held up a hand. "Hold on," he said. "Start from the beginning. We're listening."

Ben let Badger do the talking and listened, nodding, as his friend described what had happened on shore. As he spoke, he saw the Captain look increasingly worried.

"So you see," said Badger when he had reached the end of his tale. "When Mike was wrongly accused of stealing, I think he decided to go off and sign up on Bert Thorn's boat."

The Captain winced. "You say he was wrongly accused, but those items were found in his locker."

"He can't have taken them, sir," said Badger. "We were both with him all the time."

"What do you think, Mr Rigger?"

Mr Rigger fingered his moustache. "I think these boys might be right," he said. "And, frankly, I wouldn't be surprised if those things had been planted."

Captain Macbeth thought for a moment. "I must admit I felt very uneasy myself," he said at last. He sighed. "Oh dear, I'm afraid I've done that boy a great injustice. We must find him."

"But how?" asked Mr Rigger.

Badger felt that he could help. "I think we know where Bert Thorn sails to," he said. "We were told that he goes to a place called Shark Island."

The Captain scratched his head. "Shark Island? I don't think I've ever heard of it. Have you, Mr Rigger?"

Mr Rigger had not. "These islands are sometimes known by many different names," he said. "But, no, I've never heard of any Shark Island."

Ben had an idea. "Couldn't we follow Bert Thorn's ship?" he asked.

The Captain thought about this. "I doubt if he'd take kindly to that.'

"Radar," said Ben. "The *Tobermory* has radar, doesn't she?"

"Yes," said Mr Rigger. "We have radar ..." His voice tailed off. And then, his eyes sparkling, he exclaimed, "I see what you mean. We can track him on our radar while keeping just far enough away from him that he doesn't notice us. What an excellent idea!"

"Good thinking, Mr Rigger," said the Captain, and then, hastily correcting himself, "I mean, good thinking, MacTavish, B." He paused. "As long as Thorn hasn't already left."

"I don't think he has," said Badger. "If you look over at the harbour, you'll see his ship, the *Barracuda*. It's just preparing to sail. We still have time to follow it."

"All right," said the Captain. "I'll go and take a look." He paused, as if in doubt. "But what do you think we should do if we find Mike on board when they get to this Shark Island, wherever that is?"

Badger had his answer at the ready. "We'll make contact with him," he said. "We'll get a message to him somehow that he's no longer accused of theft. And ..." He did not finish.

"And?" asked the Captain.

"And we can also see what Shark Island has to hide," he said. "You see, sir, it might have something to do with Mike's father's disappearance."

The Captain thought about this for a moment. Then he said, "And I'd certainly welcome the chance to bring our friend Mr Thorn to justice."

"No friend of ours," said Mr Rigger.

"No, indeed," said the Captain. "But then sometimes you call people you really don't like your friends. They're not *real* friends, of course. You do understand that, don't you, MacTavish and Tomkins?"

"Of course," said Badger, smiling. Then he added. "And thank you, sir, and thank you, Mr Rigger. Thank you for wanting to help our friend ..."

"Our *real* friend," interjected Ben.

"You're welcome," said the Captain.

"Indeed, yes," said Mr Rigger. "So let's get ready to sail. I'll turn the radar on so that we can track the *Barracuda*."

"Good," said the Captain. "All hands on deck, Mr Rigger."

"He told me they found the sextant and the compass in my locker..."

"So let's get ready to sail. I'll turn the radar on so that we can track the *Barracuda*," said Mr Rigger.

SCHOOL SHIP TOBERMORY

The *Tobermory* dropped her great anchor in the waters of a quiet bay.

"Aye, aye, sir," said Mr Rigger, as he swung into action.

The *Barracuda* was a well-equipped and fast sailing vessel, capable of just a bit more speed than the *Tobermory*. But to do her maximum speed she required to be handled skilfully – and that was something that was beyond Bert Thorn, who, like all pirates, was a sloppy sailor. So the *Tobermory* was able to keep up with the *Barracuda* and stay just out of her sight. This required a steady and experienced hand at the wheel, so Captain Macbeth took personal charge.

They sailed through the day and it was almost dark when they spotted land up ahead. Checking the navigation chart he had brought up to the helm, the Captain saw that they were approaching a group of small islands. There were five of them, all named after birds – Eagle Island, Albatross Island, Swallow Island, Penguin Island and Blackbird Island. None of them was called Shark Island.

But then Badger suddenly noticed something as he glanced over at the Captain's chart. "Do you remember the shape of the island on Captain Tommy's chart – the one that was called Shark Island?" he said.

Thomas remembered, having had a good look at the chart when they had first taken it out of Captain

Tommy's sea-chest. "It was very narrow at the bottom and broad at the top," he said."

Badger nodded. "Yes," he said, "that's exactly how it was. And there was a long beach up at the top, wasn't there? A beach with quicksand?"

Thomas agreed that this was so. He looked more closely at the Captain's chart, still unfolded before them. As he did so, Badger leaned forward. "Captain," he said, "would you mind if I turned your chart upside down?"

The Captain looked surprised. "Why would you want to do that, Tomkins?"

"Because ..." began Badger, leaning further forward and turning the chart through one hundred and eighty degrees. "Because if you look at it this way ..."

"Shark Island!" exclaimed Thomas, pointing to the island marked on the chart as Eagle Island. "Look, it's exactly the right shape."

"And there's the beach and the river," said Badger. "And there's the volcano. So, you see, Captain Tommy's old chart was drawn accurately enough but ... upside down!"

"To confuse people," said Thomas, his voice rising in excitement.

Mr Rigger had been alerted by the hubbub and had now joined them. He and the Captain examined the chart and agreed that Badger was quite right.

"The radar screen is showing the *Barracuda* heading to Eagle Island," said Mr Rigger. "So I think we should let him carry on there. We can anchor here." He indicated Albatross Island, which was only a short distance from Eagle Island. "Then we can see what he's up to tomorrow."

The Captain agreed. "There's a nice little anchorage right here," he said, pointing to a place on the chart. "From there we'll get a very good view of Eagle ... I mean, Shark, Island."

He swung the wheel until the ship was on the right course, and just as night descended, the *Tobermory* nosed her way into the shelter of Albatross Island and dropped her great anchor in the waters of a quiet bay. They were just in time – anchoring in the darkness can be difficult and sometimes dangerous. They were safe though, their anchor dug firmly into the sand of the sea bed, holding them exactly where they wanted to be until morning came and it was time for the next stage of their adventure.

At dinner in the mess hall that night, the friends were all seated at the same table when William Edward Hardtack and Geoffrey Shark sauntered over towards them.

"Right, everybody," muttered Poppy under her breath. "Don't let them get under your skin. Just stay cool."

Hardtack smiled – a sneering, mocking smile. His nose, though, was still swollen from where he had been punched by Mike.

"So where's your friend?" he asked. "Looks like he's gone missing, doesn't it?"

Poppy looked up from her plate of spaghetti. "If you're referring to Mike," she said. "He's decided to take a break."

"Ha!" mocked Hardtack. "Is that what you call it? Taking a break? Well, there's another word for it, you know, and that's desertion. You can also call it jumping ship – but whatever you say it amounts to the same thing."

"Yes," said Shark. "And you know how that used to be punished back in the old days? I won't tell you, because it might put you off your dinner."

Hardtack was enjoying himself. "Of course I knew he wouldn't last long," he said. "That's right, isn't it, Sharky? Didn't I say to you that sort of guy will never have what it takes to be a proper sailor. Oh yes, he can row around in some little dinghy and catch fish for his mum and all that, but he will never make a real sailor."

"Out of his depth," said Shark. "People like that should know their place. They should stay where they are – on some sad little island somewhere."

Fee found it difficult to control herself. "He's twice as good as you are, Hardtack," she muttered.

"And you too, Shark."

Hardtack spun round. "Did I hear somebody say something? Oh, it's you, MacTavish, F. So you think he's as good as Sharky and me, do you? Well, I've got news for you. He's a thief. He's nothing but a common thief."

"And like all thieves, he's run away," said Shark.

"That's right, Sharky," agreed Hardtack. "And it's very fortunate that he has. The last thing you want on a ship is a thief."

This was too much for Badger. Rising to his feet, he said to Hardtack, "Listen, Hardtack. You'd better be careful who you call a thief. We know your friend Flubber planted the sextant and compass in Mike's locker. And if he's involved so are you and your pal Shark."

Hardtack made a dismissive gesture. "Oh we are, are we? And I suppose you've got proof of that."

Badger hesitated, but only for the briefest moment. Then he said, "As a matter of fact, we might. Has it occurred to you that somebody might have actually seen Flubber go into his cabin with the sextant and compass?"

Badger was watching Hardtack's expression closely as he said this, and he saw a sudden flicker of unease pass over the bully's face. And this was enough to confirm what they all thought, though it was not proof of course, because no one had really seen Flubber take the sextant and compass into the cabin he shared with Mike.

"Who? Who saw him?" stuttered Hardtack. "It's a lie – just a lie."

"Is it?" asked Badger.

Geoffrey Shark opened his mouth to say something, but was taken aside by Hardtack, who whispered something into his ear. Then the two of them moved away, shooting a furious glance at Badger as they went.

"That sorted them out," said Poppy.

"Well done, Badger," said Fee. "But who saw Flubber?"

Badger smiled. "Nobody," he said. "But they don't know that, do they?"

Ben frowned. He did not like the idea of telling a lie – ever. But then he thought again. What had Badger actually said? He remembered his precise words: *Has it occurred to you that somebody might have actually seen him?*

Badger had never claimed that somebody had seen Flubber. He had really just asked them whether they thought somebody might have seen him. That was a very different thing.

And there was something troubling Poppy. Hardtack had talked about Mike being nothing but a common thief, but how did he know that the compass and sextant were missing? There had been no public announcement of this, and yet he knew, which suggested that if anybody was a thief, then it was him – or one of his friends. She wondered whether she could make something of this, but decided not to. It was always difficult with Hardtack and his gang: you never seemed to have the proof you needed. They were as slippery as eels, she thought, although she did not wish to be unfair to eels ...

CHAPTER 15

A message from Mike

Ben was glad to get up the following morning. He had not slept well, and his dreams had actually been nightmares. In one of them he was being pursued across a beach by Bert Thorn, who was waving a cutlass in the air and shouting terrible threats. In another he was tied up right down at the bottom of the ship in the bilges and water was coming in fast through a hole. When you wake up from dreams like that, you are always pleased to discover yourself in one piece and safe in your bed – or hammock, in Ben's case.

At muster call that morning, Mr Rigger told Ben, Fee and their Middle Deck friends to stay behind to get special instructions. Everybody else, he said, was to carry on with their normal routine, as the ship would stay at anchor all day.

A lot of people groaned. The bay was just right for snorkelling, with clear blue water and a sea bed of pure white sand, yet most of them would be cooped up in the classrooms.

"You seven," Mr Rigger said, addressing Ben, Fee, Badger, Thomas, Poppy, Tanya and Angela, "have been put on special duties with me."

"Why them?" complained Shark. "What have they done to deserve special duties when we have to sit in the classroom? It's not fair, sir!"

Mr Rigger told Shark that it was none of his business.

The reason why they had all been chosen for special duties was of course that Ben and Badger had been the ones to pass on the information about Mike signing up on Bert Thorn's ship. As their close friends, Poppy, Fee, Tanya and Angela could obviously be trusted and relied on to help them in finding out what had happened to Mike. And Thomas Seagrape was chosen because he knew his way around Caribbean islands and would be a valuable part of the team.

Drawing them all aside, Mr Rigger explained what he and the Captain had in mind. "We think that the best thing to do is to keep a close watch on the *Barracuda*. Captain Macbeth is going to let you use his best telescope – you can set it up on the deck."

Angela and Fee went to fetch the telescope from the Captain's cabin and soon had it set up in a position that gave them an uninterrupted view of the bay on Shark Island where the *Barracuda* lay at anchor.

It was not long before they saw that there was a great deal of activity on the other ship. "They're unloading something," said Angela as she peered through the powerful lens of the telescope. "They're lowering things into a large rowing boat."

"What sort of things?" asked Poppy.

Angela struggled to make out the details. "I can't really tell," she said. "Some boxes and … yes, that looks like a set of oars and … and yes, some cans of fuel, I think."

They took it in turns to look through the telescope. Fee saw the crew of the *Barracuda* unloading some machinery and several large sacks. Poppy saw the rowing boat make the short journey to shore, transfer its cargo onto a jetty, and then return to the *Barracuda* for more. And then it was Tanya's turn. She saw the crew climb down a ladder and board a motor boat which then shot off, leaving, as far as she could make out, only one figure on the deck.

It was Thomas who identified who it was when it was his turn to look through the telescope. "That's Mike!" he shouted. "It looks like he's the only person left on board."

Fee ran off to tell Mr Rigger, who rushed back to see for himself. "Yes," he said, as he trained the telescope on the distant ship. "That looks like him all right. And it does seem as if he's all alone."

"What should we do?" asked Poppy. "Should we go over there?"

Mr Rigger looked thoughtful. Twiddling his moustache – a sure sign that he was thinking hard – he said, "What if the *Barracuda*'s crew suddenly come back? We wouldn't want a show-down, would we?"

Badger had an idea. "Mike knows all about signalling flags," he said. "If we send a message, he should be able to see it, even from this distance."

Mr Rigger thought that this was an excellent idea. "Fetch the flags," he said to Ben. "We'll run some up right away."

They made the first message a brief one. Selecting the flags for the letters M, I, K and E, they ran them up on a long line that rose right to the top of the mast and fluttered in the breeze. With bated breath they waited for a response.

"I don't think he's seen them," said Angela, who had resumed her post at the telescope. "He's just standing there, doing nothing."

But then she reported excitedly, "No, he's not, he's … yes, he's putting up some flags."

Now there was complete silence as they waited for Angela to decipher the message spelt out by the flags Mike had raised on the deck of the *Barracuda*. "He says …YES," she said.

Turning to Badger, Mr Rigger gave his order. "Put this message up," he said. "WHAT DO YOU

WANT US TO DO?"

Up went the colourful flags, and after a few minutes Angela read out the answering message. "MEET ME ON THE BEACH TONIGHT AT NINE."

A buzz of excitement ran through the group as a host of questions crowded through their minds. What had Mike discovered? Was he in danger? How would he get from the *Barracuda* to the beach? If he could get to the beach, could he get back to the *Tobermory* itself?

Mr Rigger sent the final message himself. "WILL DO," he signalled.

There was something that Poppy was keen to ask. "Can we all go?" she asked.

Mr Rigger hesitated. Then he gave his answer. "I don't see why not," he said. "But keep it to yourselves. I don't want news of this getting out. Understand?"

They all nodded. "We'll keep it strictly secret," said Tanya. "We promise."

"Good," said Mr Rigger. "So off you all go to class now and report back to me after dinner. Eight-thirty sharp. And wear something dark. We don't want to be spotted by anyone."

At exactly half past eight, while everybody else was busy down below, the group assembled by one of the liberty boat stations on the top deck. Mr Rigger was there in dark clothing and without his customary white cap. Although it was already twilight, there was a half-moon which shed a certain amount of light and they would have to be careful, he said, not to be visible. All the others were wearing dark clothing too, just as he had instructed them.

As stealthily as they could they lowered one of the liberty boats into the water and then climbed down a rope ladder to board it. Poppy and Thomas were the best rowers, so they each took charge of an oar while the others crouched down behind the sides of the boat.

"Cast off," whispered Mr Rigger as he took control of the tiller.

Silently Poppy and Thomas dipped their oars into the water and began to pull. Their skill paid off: hardly a splash could be heard as the blades of the oars slipped into the sea and propelled them away from the *Tobermory* towards the shore of Shark Island. They gave a wide berth to the *Barracuda*, on which a few lights could be seen shining from portholes. There was no sign of life on the other ship and it looked like no watch had been posted to keep a look-out.

"They'll be down below drinking rum," whispered Mr Rigger. "That's what pirates do." He shook his head in disapproval. "Useless bunch – not a single good sailor amongst the lot of them. Just drinking and noisy parties and stealing – that's all they're good for."

It didn't take them long to reach the beach, where they dragged their boat up from the edge of the water to keep it from drifting away with the tide.

It had become darker, as the moon had retreated behind a cloud. Gathering them all around him, Mr Rigger explained that they should split into three groups and keep watch at various points on the beach for Mike. "If you meet him," he said, "whistle like this and we'll come to you." He gave a sample whistle; Ben thought that it sounded very like one of the shore birds that you see chasing after the retreating wavelets; Fee thought that it sounded very much like somebody trying to sound like a bird; and Badger thought that it sounded just like somebody trying to let people know that they had met up with somebody they had been hoping to meet up with. He did not say this, though, and simply nodded like everybody else to acknowledge Mr Rigger's instruction.

Fee, Poppy and Tanya were all in one group, led by Poppy. They made their way as quietly as possible down to the end of the beach. Mangrove trees grew here – those trees with their strange, finger-like roots that dip their way into the edge of the sea and seem not to mind the salt water. Mr Rigger had told them not to use a torch, so they could not see very well. Poppy narrowly avoided tripping up over a mangrove root and Tanya scraped her shin on a rock. But they eventually reached the end of the beach and sat down on the sand to keep a look-out for Mike. It was now five minutes to nine, which meant that if he was coming, he would be there at any moment.

And Mike was as good as his word. Precisely at nine, Fee announced that she could hear something. "I heard a splash," she whispered. "I'm sure I did."

They all looked out to sea, straining their eyes in the darkness. And then, as if responding to an unspoken plea, the moon came out from behind a cloud, and there was Mike, nosing a kayak onto the beach in front of them.

It took a real effort not to shout out a welcome. "Mike!" hissed Poppy. "We're over here."

Tanya was first to reach him, and helped him to drag the kayak up onto the sand. There they clustered round him, while Poppy gave the agreed signal to let the others know that Mike had arrived. In no time, everybody else had converged to welcome their friend.

"Don't waste any time," said Mr Rigger, his voice lowered to little more than a whisper. "Tell us what happened."

Mike started his story without delay. "I signed up as a cabin boy," he said.

"Why did you do it? asked Mr Rigger.

Mike hesitated. "I was accused of ..."

Mr Rigger stopped him. "I'm sorry. We know now

the theft of the items from Captain Tommy's sea-chest had nothing to do with you."

They could see that Mike was relieved by this. "Good," he said, smiling broadly. "Anyway, there was another reason. You know all about my father's disappearance?"

"Yes," said Mr Rigger.

"Well," said Mike. "Well, there's something that Ben, Badger, Thomas and I heard when we went ashore that made me think he might be here on Shark Island. I also thought that Bert Thorn might be mixed up in it in some way."

"And is he?" asked Mr Rigger.

Mike nodded. "I don't know for sure yet. But I do know that the woman in the coconut bar was right. Thorn brings in supplies and takes them inland. And then he brings out large crates. They're making something there in some kind of secret factory."

There was a long silence as they thought about this. What on earth could people be making in the middle of a remote island? It would have to be something very secret for them to go to such enormous trouble.

Mr Rigger cleared his throat. "Well, you've found out something very important, Mike. It was a risky thing to do, but you've done it. Now you can come back to the *Tobermory* with us. It's up to the authorities to take things further."

Mike shook his head. "Please, Mr Rigger. Please let me see this through. If this is all somehow connected with my father, this might be my only chance to find out what happened to him."

Mr Rigger frowned. "But what do you suggest we do?" he asked.

They all watched Mike as he revealed his plan. It was bold, and it was dangerous, but not one of them wanted to turn back.

"I managed to listen in to a conversation between Bert Thorn and one of his crew," said Mike. "They didn't realise I could hear, but they were discussing the route inland.

"The crewman said that there was a footbridge that needed repairing, and the rest of the track was also in a bad state." He paused. "The track starts just over there," he said, pointing to some mangrove trees.

Mr Rigger looked uncertain. "And what do we do when we get to the factory – *if* we get there?"

Mike was ready for the question. "There's a cook on the *Barracuda* who told me earlier about going to this place once with some other members of the crew. He said the secret factory is on an island in the middle of a lagoon which connects with the sea, and that the lagoon is full of sharks. The people who work in the factory have all been kidnapped, and Thorn keeps them there like prisoners. The sharks are his main security, as anyone trying to escape would be

eaten alive if they tried to swim across the lagoon. And of course the sharks also keep nosey people out. But he also said that there's a way of crossing safely. If you throw fish into the water a little way away from where you want to cross, it distracts the sharks and they'll be too busy eating to notice you wading across."

"But where are we going to get fish?" asked Ben.

Mike had expected this question too and answered quickly. "The cook said they keep a barrel of it on each side of the lagoon."

Mr Rigger shook his head. "I'm not having it," he said. "I'm not going to have anyone risking their lives swimming through shark-infested waters. And anyway, I'm not sure that we should get mixed up in all this."

Mike pleaded with him. "Please, Mr Rigger," he begged. "If there's any chance – even the smallest one – of finding out about my father, I have to take it."

Badger added his support. "Please, sir," he said. "It means such a lot to him."

And so did Poppy: "Please, Mr Rigger. Please help Mike. It's his only chance."

Mr Rigger was clearly torn. On the one hand he was an officer of the *Tobermory*, responsible for the safety of his students and under a duty to ensure they didn't get into any unnecessary danger. On the other hand, he was a kind man who clearly understood what this opportunity meant to Mike.

"I'm not sure …" he began.

Poppy sensed his uncertainty. "We all really want to help Mike," she pleaded. "And we know how kind you are, Mr Rigger. We know you want to help him too."

That was the final nudge he needed, and he gave in. "Very well," he said. "Time's getting on. I think we should set off."

It didn't take them long to get to the track behind the mangroves. It was a broad, well-worn path, but very uneven. Fee led the way, because she had the best night vision, and was able to spot any obstacles better than anybody else. Close behind her came Mr Rigger, and behind him was Poppy and the others. At the rear was Badger, who looked behind them every so often just to make sure they were not being followed.

After they had walked for a few minutes they came to the footbridge Mike had mentioned. It was a very narrow bridge, slung between two sides of a deep ravine. "Be careful not to tread on one of these—" began Fee, and immediately stood herself on one of the rotten planks. With an awful cracking sound the wood gave way beneath her, and her leg slipped down into the void below. Far beneath them – a good hundred feet – a river tumbled down towards the sea. Fee was shaking as she felt Mr Rigger hoist her back onto her feet. "Careful!" he whispered. "Take it slowly, Fee."

They eventually reached the other side. From there it was downhill through thick jungle before the path came to the shore of the lagoon. There in the centre was a small island on which they could see a large building surrounded by a ring of wooden cabins.

For a few minutes the whole party just stood and gazed at the sight, which was now quite clearly visible in the moonlight. But there was no time to waste, and Mr Rigger urged them on towards the edge of the water.

Mike looked about him, searching in the darkness for the barrel of fish. He didn't notice it at first, but then he saw it, just a short distance away, half-concealed by a bush.

"Look! There's the barrel. I'll go and get some fish," he said.

He was away for only a moment and when he returned he was shaking his head. "It's empty," he said. "It smelled of fish all right, but it's empty. They must have used it all up and haven't got round to filling it again."

"So we'll have to cross over without using anything to distract the sharks," said Badger. "That's not much use, is it?"

"Only one person needs to cross," said Mike. "Then he – or she – can go and distract the sharks with fish from the other barrel to let all the others get across."

"And what happens if the other barrel is empty too? No, it's far too dangerous," said Mr Rigger. "There's no alternative but to turn back, I'm afraid."

Mike pleaded. "But we're so close now. We can't turn back. I'll swim across."

Mr Rigger shook his head. "No, I'm sorry, I won't allow it." He paused and thought for a moment. "But that's not to say that I won't allow *myself* to go. In fact, I have just given myself permission. I'll do it."

"No, you can't, sir," said Mike. "Please let me."

But Mr Rigger would not be persuaded otherwise.

They had to walk a little bit further to find the narrowest part of the lagoon. On the island opposite they could make out a small shack thatched with old banana tree fronds, with what looked like a barrel beside it.

"That's our place," said Mr Rigger, as he stepped into the water. "Be very careful, sir," whispered Badger.

Mr Rigger said nothing, but began to swim as quietly as he could across the brief divide of water.

And it was then that Badger saw a dark triangular shape moving through the water, heading straight for Mr Rigger. The sight made his heart miss a beat, then thump wildly, as it will often do after you see something really frightening and dangerous.

Badger opened his mouth to shout a warning, but no sound came.

CHAPTER 16

Reunited at last

Badger had to act quickly. But what could he do? He had never been in a situation like this, and he felt completely helpless.

And then it came to him, and he knew exactly what he had to do. Mr Rigger was in the water; the shark was in the water; he, Badger, would go into the water too …

"What are you doing, Badger?" Ben asked. "You can't go in!"

But that was exactly what he did. With a great lunge Badger launched himself into the black waters of the lagoon and began to splash about for all his worth. His friends watched in astonishment as he floundered and thrashed about in the shallows, venturing in as far as his waist, his arms beating at the surface, making as much disturbance as possible. Why on earth had he chosen this moment of all to start playing around in the water? they asked themselves.

And then they saw what he was doing. The shark's

fin, which had been cutting through the water in wide circles round Mr Rigger, suddenly stopped moving. Then it turned, pointing directly at Badger and, slowly at first, began to move towards the new source of disturbance. Badger had deliberately drawn the shark's attention away from Mr Rigger towards himself.

Sharks are inquisitive creatures: if there is something going on in the water, they want to know all about it. No shark could have resisted the temptation to investigate the splashing that was taking place by the edge of the lagoon. It could be some tasty creature in difficulty, after all – just the sort of thing a shark might enjoy for a late-night snack.

By now Mr Rigger was close to the other side, and in a few seconds he was there, striding out of the water on the island side. Seeing this, Badger realised it was time for him to get out of the water himself. With an eye on the shark's fin, which was getting closer and closer, he began to make his way back to the shore. It was slow going, as wading through water is not easy, even if it only comes up to your waist. And the fin, he saw when he glanced over his shoulder, was moving faster and faster.

"Hurry up!" shouted Ben from the shore.

"Come on, Badger!" yelled Poppy. "Quick, quick!"

Ben saw that the shark was gaining quickly on his friend. Looking around desperately for something that might distract the shark a second time, he noticed that the shore was littered with large pebbles. He bent down to pick one up and hurled it with all his strength into the water. Ben knew that it might not do much good, but at least it would be something. It worked. As soon as the pebble splashed into the lagoon, the shark turned from its course slightly. It was not for long, but it was enough, and Badger, by now in very shallow water, managed to stagger onto the beach. He was safe.

He had seen what Ben had done with the pebble. It had probably saved his life, but there was no time for thanks now. There would be plenty of opportunity for that later. Right now all of them watched as Mr Rigger made his way to the barrel of fish, turned it on its side, rolled it down to the edge of the lagoon a good few hundred yards along the shore, and emptied its contents into the water. "I'm starting the feeding frenzy," he called to them.

Suddenly the water was a boiling mass of activity as all the sharks thrashed around, snapping up each morsel of food. Further back, on the opposite shore, the group of friends began to cross the lagoon. They did so in safety, as the sharks were all busy elsewhere, but it was still frightening going into a stretch of water where only a short while ago they had seen a shark circling. But they did it, and a few minutes later they were on the other side, dripping wet, proud of themselves and ready for what lay ahead.

Mr Rigger came back to join them. He had not seen the shark, nor realised the extent of the danger he had been in. But when Poppy told him what had happened he wiped his brow with relief.

"Thank you, Badger," he said. "I believe you saved my life."

But Badger did not want to make much of it. "Actually, Ben saved mine," he said.

"Well, whatever happened, I'm proud of you all," said Mr Rigger. "But now we need to get moving and find out what's going on here."

Walking as quietly as is possible in boots full of water, Mr Rigger led the small group towards the first of the cabins surrounding the main building.

"We need to take a look in there," he whispered. "Badger and Tanya, you come with me. The rest of you stay here and keep quiet."

Mr Rigger and his two assistants detached themselves from the group and crept towards the cabin. When they reached it, he very gently tried the door. It was not locked, and it opened without a squeak. The three of them went in, walking as lightly as they could in case there were any loose floorboards that might give them away.

There were none, but with each step he took, the water in Mr Rigger's boots made a strange gurgling, squelching sound. At first this was not too obvious, but then it became louder and louder. Mr Rigger stopped, and looked down helplessly at his boots. And it was then that the flashlight was switched on.

They stood stock still, caught in the blinding beam of light.

"Who are you? Why are you here?" asked a voice.

Mr Rigger coughed. "We're lost," he said. "We came ashore to have a look around and can't find our way back."

The light moved, shining on each of their faces in turn, before it was pointed away towards the floor. Now the three intruders could see who was talking to them.

It was a man wearing a shabby pair of red pyjamas. He had a beard and a shock of unkempt hair, and his face had a sad and weary look to it.

"So you're not from the *Barracuda*?" said the man, obviously confused.

"No," said Mr Rigger.

The man stepped towards them. "Then you're … you're strangers?"

"You could call us that," said Mr Rigger.

This answer seemed to worry the man. "You're in real danger then," he said. "You shouldn't be here. If they find you …"

"Hold on," interrupted Mr Rigger. "What do you mean? Why should we be in danger?"

"I'll explain," said the man, gesturing for them to

go with him into a small room off the main part of the cabin. There was a table here with a few chairs around it, and they all sat down.

"This place," he began, "is run by a man called Bert Thorn. He's a terrible man. I'm not sure what you'd call him. I suppose pirate might be the word. Anyway, he built a factory here that makes fake goods – you know, forgeries. People are always prepared to pay a lot for things that they think are worth something – expensive watches, designer jeans and so on. Well, this is where they make a lot of cheap versions of expensive goods. Thorn then sells them off as the real thing and makes a fortune in the process."

Mr Rigger nodded.

"Or should I say," the man went on, "this is where *we* make a lot of that stuff. You see, if you can get people to work for nothing – if you don't have to pay them – you make even more money."

Mr Rigger gasped. "That happens here?"

"Yes. There are about twenty of us. We were kidnapped by Thorn and brought here to work. And they work us hard – seven days a week, with only a couple of hours off. Some of us have been here for years."

"And you couldn't escape?" asked Tanya.

The man turned to her and spoke sadly. "No. We can't get off the island because of the sharks. They keep us in – and keep any visitors out. That was why

I was so surprised to see you." He sighed. "We've seen how Thorn and his men get across the lagoon themselves, but the barrels of fish they use are usually locked away – except when Thorn's ship is in the bay. And there'd be no point in our getting to the beach when they're anchored off it."

For a while there was silence as they took in what the man had said. Then Mr Rigger spoke. "Is there someone here who disappeared in Dominica a few years ago?"

The man nodded. "There are two of them," he answered.

"And one of them has a son called Mike?"

The man smiled. "Yes, he does," he said enthusiastically. "He's often spoken about the boy."

"Where is he?" asked Mr Rigger.

"The cabin next door," said the man. "But you'd better not stay here any longer. If Thorn's men catch you here you'll end up prisoners like us."

Mr Rigger spoke hurriedly to the man. "Listen carefully," he said. "We're leaving all right. We can't take everyone, but there will be room for two. So if you want to get out of here …"

"I do," said the man.

"Then get ready," instructed Mr Rigger.

While the man quickly got dressed, Mr Rigger, Ben and Tanya left the cabin and retraced their steps to join the others.

"What's happening?" asked Fee. "Did you find anybody?"

Mr Rigger nodded. "I'll explain in due course," he said, "but for the moment I want Mike to come with me."

Mike stepped forward. "Where are we going?" he asked.

Mr Rigger pointed to the second cabin. "We're going in there," he said.

"Why?" asked Mike.

"You'll find out," said Mr Rigger.

He could have told the boy what to expect, but he decided not to. There are some things that are better left as surprises, and he knew this would be one of them.

Again the door of the cabin didn't resist when Mr Rigger pushed it. Once inside, he edged forward in the darkness saying, quite loudly, "Don't be afraid. Wake up. Don't be afraid. We're friends."

There was a muffled sound, and then a small bedside lamp was turned on. There in a rough, low-slung bed was a man wearing a tee-shirt and a pair of striped sailing trousers. He had been fast asleep, and was rubbing his eyes in confusion.

Mike could scarcely believe his eyes. With a cry he rushed forward. "Dad!" he sobbed. "Dad, it's me. It's Mike."

Mr Rigger turned away and left the cabin. This

was a private moment, something special for Mike and his father, and he wanted them to experience it together, without his looking on.

After a few minutes he came back in to see Mike's father had got out of the bed and was holding his son in an embrace so tight that even a tractor wouldn't have been able to pull them apart. Both were weeping – but their tears, he could tell, were tears of joy.

"Quick! We don't have much time," Mr Rigger said. "Mike, help your father to get ready and then come outside and join us. We're getting out of here."

When everybody was assembled outside, Mr Rigger gave the signal to leave. They walked as quietly as they could, and nobody heard them, although at one point a dog started to bark. Mr Rigger was worried this might raise the alarm, but Mike's father explained that the dogs often barked at night for no reason, and the guards, who lived in the last of the cabins, were far too lazy to investigate.

Within a few minutes they were all standing near the edge of the lagoon. Mike's father offered to throw the fish into the water to distract the sharks, and Mike said that he would help him. "We'll come after you," Mike said. "Start crossing once we let you know that the sharks are busy."

The plan worked perfectly. The sharks were pleased to have a second meal so short a time after their first, and there was a great swirling in the water as they gobbled up their treat. While the sharks were busy, the group swam across the lagoon, reaching the other side rather more quickly than it had taken them to cross before. Then, shaking the water out of their shoes as best they could, they followed the path back towards the shore.

They made it over the bridge without incident and after a few more minutes found themselves approaching the sand dunes at the edge of the beach. And it was here that they heard the cries.

Fee heard them first. "What's that?" she asked.

Poppy listened. "I can't hear anything," she said. "Maybe it's a bird. An owl, perhaps."

"No," said Fee. "It was voices."

This time the voices were louder – and clearer – and it was easy enough to make out what they said.

"Help!" cried a voice.

"Help us!" shouted another.

"Please, please help!" came the cry of a third.

Mr Rigger started to run in the direction from which the cries were coming, and all the others followed him. From the dunes, they looked down on the moonlit beach and saw in a moment of complete astonishment, three people in the sand – or rather three *half*-people, because whoever they were appeared to be partially buried.

Badger realised immediately what was happening.

"They're in the quicksand," he shouted.

Mr Rigger took control. "Right, everybody," he said, "follow me, but don't, whatever you do, get too close to the quicksand. Understand?"

They approached carefully and were soon close enough to make out the faces of the three people stuck in the sand.

"It's Hardtack!" exclaimed Poppy.

"And Shark," said Fee.

"And Flubber," added Ben.

The three boys were desperately squirming and struggling, pleading for help. "Keep still!" shouted Mr Rigger. "The more you struggle, the more the sand will suck you down."

The three terrified boys immediately stopped writhing. Looking about him, Mr Rigger saw Mike's kayak lying on the beach.

"Ben and Badger, go and get the kayak," he ordered. "We'll push it out over the quicksand – they'll be able to grab hold of it."

It was a good plan. After pushing the kayak over towards Hardtack, Ben and Badger waited until he had a firm grip on its prow before very slowly dragging the trapped boy out of the sand. When he finally emerged with a strange, squelching, popping sound, they all wanted to cheer, but stopped themselves, as Mr Rigger had told them all to remain silent. Then it was Shark's turn, and finally Flubber's.

Mr Rigger looked at the three mud-caked boys,

his expression one of severe disapproval. "What are you doing here?" he asked.

Hardtack spoke for all three. "We only wanted to find out what was going on," he said. "We didn't expect to find quicksand here."

"The map said it was at the top of the island," said Shark. "Look, here it is …" And with that he took Captain Tommy's now soaking map from his pocket and unfolded it. Then he realised what he had done; but it was too late. Hardtack gave him a withering look, and Flubber rolled his eyes.

"You didn't know it was upside down," said Ben. "You thought this beach was at the other side of the island."

"So you stole the map after all," said Poppy. "You had it all along."

"I don't know what Geoffrey's talking about," said Hardtack quickly. "I've never seen that map in my life."

"We'll talk about that later," said Mr Rigger, giving Hardtack an accusing look. "In the meantime, get into your boat and follow us back to the *Tobermory*." He paused. "And once you've had a shower to get all that mud off you, go straight to your cabins and remain there until first thing tomorrow morning, when you are to report to the Captain.'

Hardtack and his friends did not like the sound of this at all, but they knew better than to argue with

Mr Rigger. Everybody got into the other boat, and Mike left the kayak on the shore – he had borrowed it from the *Barracuda* and they could come and get it themselves.

Back on the *Tobermory* everybody was too tired to do anything other than get into their hammocks and go straight to sleep. Cabins were found for Mike's father and the other man from the island, and they were soon comfortably settled in. For Mike, though, there was one task to do before he went off to his hammock, and that was to send an urgent message to Antigua to say that his father had been found safe and sound.

That done, he went off to join Ben and Badger in their cabin, Mr Rigger having told him to move his hammock there so he wouldn't have to share with the disgraced Maximilian Flubber. Mike was very pleased to do this, though by the time he had slung his hammock across a corner of his friends' cabin, Ben and Badger were fast asleep, so he had nobody to chat to before he drifted off. But he had enough happy thoughts to keep him occupied as he went to sleep. He had found his father; he had been cleared of theft; he had even helped to save Hardtack and his friends from that perilous quicksand. There was a lot to be happy with, indeed to feel very proud of.

He wondered what he would dream about that night. Would it be sharks? He hoped not. Would it be quicksand? Again, he hoped not. He need not have worried, because his dreams featured neither of these things. Instead they were about being with his father, on a boat somewhere at sea, looking at the sun on the water and feeling happier than he had ever felt before.

The next morning the *Tobermory* left her anchorage on the morning tide. There was no sign of any activity on the *Barracuda*, where the crew, it would seem, were all still asleep. Captain Macbeth was happy to get away before the other ship came to life, as his main concern was to get to Guadeloupe as soon as he possibly could and notify the police about the *Barracuda* and Bert Thorn's activities on Shark Island.

Mr Rigger had told him the whole story, and Captain Macbeth was delighted there was enough evidence to put before the authorities. If all went well, the French navy, who had a patrol boat stationed on Guadeloupe, would soon be off to Shark Island to free the remaining captives and arrest Bert Thorn.

But there were other, more immediate, things he had to do, and he lost no time in dealing with William Edward Hardtack and his friends.

"You know very well it's against the rules to leave the ship at night without a member of staff," he said. "And yet you deliberately did so."

He asked Hardtack if there was any good reason why the three boys had gone ashore, but Hardtack could think of none.

"In that case," said the Captain. "Twenty days of cleaning the heads – for all three of you."

After dismissing them, he asked for Mike to come to his cabin.

"I owe you an apology about the missing items from Captain Tommy's chest," he said. "I shouldn't have jumped to conclusions."

"I don't blame you, Captain," said Mike. "And I accept your apology.'

"Well, that's good of you," said the Captain. "And I'm really pleased about your father. Do you think he might join us on the *Tobermory*, as Mr Rigger's assistant, for the rest of this voyage?"

"Why not ask him?" suggested Mike.

The answer, of course, was yes, and Mike's father was soon kitted out in *Tobermory* uniform and proving to be a very helpful assistant to Mr Rigger. As for the others, they were delighted that Mike had found his father, that Bert Thorn would be arrested, and that the poor people kept prisoner on Shark Island would shortly be rescued.

With everything sorted out, it was time for the *Tobermory* to continue on her way. So they soon set out, following a course due south. Before them were long, sunny days of sailing, and hour upon hour of being with friends – which is the greatest pleasure of all.

"Do you know something?" said Ben in his cabin one night as they sailed towards Dominica. "There's nowhere else I would rather be than here – right here, with you, Badger, and you, Mike."

Badger laughed. "That's a short speech, Ben," he said. "Have you anything else to add?"

Ben thought for a moment. There was so much that he wanted to say, but he was not sure he would get the right words in the right order. So he simply said nothing. But then Mike spoke.

"I've got something to say," he said.

"What is it?" asked Badger, beginning to sound drowsy.

"It's one word," said Mike. "Thanks."

Ben thought this was a great speech. It was very short, but then the best speeches always are. And there were times, he felt, when one word, one simple word, could say it all.